PRAISE FOR *THAT'S WHEN THE KNIVES COME DOWN*

"Between the moment you lose something and the moment you realize it has been lost is *That's When the Knives Come Down*. In the spirit of Donald Barthelme, Dolan Morgan queers the every day and leaves a sinister domestic scene behind."

— Catherine Lacey, author of *No One Is Ever Missing*

"Dolan Morgan's stories in *That's When the Knives Come Down* are finely wrought puzzles of humor and grief and the absurd. Read them and feel fortified."

— Manuel Gonzales, author of *The Miniature Wife*

"The multiple worlds Dolan Morgan creates sit atop a shifting, slippery, unpredictable darkness, one that means you'd better not get used to getting used to anything in these devilishly clever stories."

— Amber Sparks, author of *May We Shed These Human Bodies*

"Dolan Morgan has the might of a unique voice, and there aren't nearly as many of those as you'd think based on book blurbs. But believe this blurb. Those who do not will be dumber for it and not know why."

— Robb Todd, author of *Steal Me for Your Stories*

D0813223

T

W

T

K

C

D

Published by Aforementioned Productions. Aforementioned and AP colophon are trademarks of Aforementioned Productions, Inc.

Stories in this collection originally appeared, some in varied form, in the following journals: *Armchair/Shotgun*, *Eclectica Magazine*, *SAND Journal*, *Contrary Magazine*, *PANK*, *Vol. 1 Brooklyn*, *The Lifted Brow*, *Prick of the Spindle*, *A Thousand Words*, *apt*, *TRNSFR*, and *The Litter Box*.

ISBN: 978-0-941143-00-1

Published August 2014.

Cover art by Eric Amling.
Cover design by Alban Fischer.
Illustrations by Robin E. Mørk.
Book designed by Carissa Halston and Randolph Pfaff.

Printed in the United States of America.

aforementioned.org

A | P

THAT'S

WHEN

THE

STORIES BY DOLAN MORGAN

KNIVES

ILLUSTRATED BY ROBIN E. MØRK

COME

DOWN

For nothing.

CONTENTS

INFESTATION

It ended. A renewed military campaign, enacted in swift concert with the most powerful industrial nations, served to do away with the goats entirely in most parts. Some towns saw inclement weather or lack of local resources do the job. Others introduced predators into the streets, like lions and wolves. In any event, the goats receded. The epidemic was over. Parks, hospitals, bakeries, and barbed wire fencing—everywhere, suddenly goat-free. And the country gave out a sigh that said, "Now what?" All felt it. Whether or not someone started a new life or tried to salvage an old one, everyone was forced to live in an entirely new world without goats overrunning everything everywhere. It was overwhelming. Before the goats, people had lived in a world where not having goats everywhere wasn't worth bringing up at all—inasmuch as people don't mention not having cabanas everywhere or stopwatches or park benches—but now not having goats around defined just about everything. You could drive to work, yes, just like before the goats, though not because you always could, but because now there were no goats in the street. You could shop at the supermarket, thank god, exactly as before, though not just because farms had grown the produce and shipped it to town, but because now goats hadn't eaten it all ahead of time.

Something not being there at all is much different from something first being there and then not being there, Mr. Hunter felt, and it having been there once would always set it apart from all the other things that never were at all. His wife, Jenna, had disappeared just before the goats were vanquished. She stepped outside during a party celebrating the imminent end of the epidemic, and just like that she was gone. Or, rather, it wasn't at that exact moment that she was gone: it is always much after the last time you see someone that it truly becomes the last time you saw them. For example, at that moment, she had simply left and Mr. Hunter would definitely see her again soon—mingling at the party, getting their coats, walking in the parking lot, at the house. It was only later, after having not seen her in any of those moments, that he in fact would not see her again.

Not that Mr. Hunter didn't try to see her, he just didn't know where to look. At first he looked around the party and then in the car and then at the house and in the yard. Later, he looked behind cupboards, under carpets, around corners, through shutters, beside toolsheds, beneath floorboards, in chimneys, and everywhere he could think of over the months, yelling *Jenna, Jenna*, but Mr. Hunter was never very good

4

at solving puzzles or being loud. He imagined her in all the same nonexistent places that the goats must have gone off to because, just like them, Jenna was also not in all the places they weren't. The goats were not everywhere. You could fill an ocean with where they weren't, and more. They were not in the suburbs, not in the country, and not in the soil, not in the sewers, not in the attics, not in the basements, the closets, the ducts, the highways, the stairs, and not in delivery trucks or mailboxes. Just about anywhere, they were not. And neither was Jenna. So wherever they weren't not, Mr. Hunter thought, maybe Jenna wasn't not there as well.

Half accepting that Jenna wouldn't be found, Mr. Hunter, still desperate, tried replacing her instead with a long queue of women who were also waiting to replace something of their own. When he went to Laura's apartment after a few dates, he'd hoped that they could be like two streams or strands pouring together from nothing (but they weren't) and that it would make him happy (but it didn't). They were more like two empty photo albums trying to steal pictures from each other. It was awful and, by the end of the night, even a bit angry and violent. They scratched and hammered at each other like they were doors they could break through, though obviously they weren't, and by morning they hadn't reached the other side of anything but the night, and that only barely, so Mr. Hunter had brunch alone at an outside cafe and, hungover, watched the helicopters not hover at all anywhere and not slaughter goats anymore with the same

5

enthusiasm he didn't feel not peppering his eggs. Later that day at the copy shop, Mr. Hunter said he was ready to settle down and then threw a stapler across the room. Maybe Jenna wouldn't be replaced with a long list of women, he considered.

The Coalition, though, had begun work on replacing things all over town, signs and streets and storefronts, previously destroyed by the goats. The Coalition, an interim council during the crisis, remained in power even after the goats had been removed and, when not sleeping with each other, worked diligently on renovations and town restoration. Albert, president of the Coalition, declared, "These plans are not only for mere regular human living, but also for our new human/not-goat living," and with that began unveiling new finished projects weekly. "The structure of these gates and roads and sidewalks, originally built with paths and mechanisms to accommodate both people and goats, will remind us that the goats once were here, and these little doors next to our own doors will tell us everyday that they once may have shared the world with us if not taken it over completely. By building for them in their absence, we remind ourselves what to be thankful for," and, just like that, what had only been a constant sensation became a physical reality. People lived not just in a town, but in a fully rendered town-without-goats.

Inspired, Mr. Hunter tried the same approach with Jenna. Wherever she would have been in his life, he tried to put something there that physically made it clear. He didn't want to replace Jenna with new Jennas anymore. And he didn't want to replace Jenna with old Jennas anymore either. He wanted to replace Jenna with Jenna. When he felt like calling her cell, he did. She didn't answer, but he left voice mails to the automated message telling him the number had been disconnected. He told the recording what he did that day or what he might do the next day. When he went out to eat, he sometimes paid for an extra drink or meal, as if it were her, or let Jenna pay for his. On her birthday, he bought presents and left them unwrapped around the house. In the morning, he would wait to take a shower just long enough for her to have taken one if she needed to.

Jenna had been a Coalition member, so Mr. Hunter started attending meetings, both in memoriam and the hopes of meeting new people. He put in a lot of hard work and quickly rose in the ranks.

With his new higher positions, two things happened: 1) he gained more authority and jurisdiction over Coalition projects, and 2) he briefly dated a younger woman, Ellen. Mr. Hunter thought that something new could be formed with Ellen, a simple relationship that wouldn't disrupt his Jenna dance. They spoke on the phone only a few times before she stopped coming to meetings. Miffed, Mr. Hunter dealt with it by simply incorporating Ellen into his growing Jenna routine. He rode the bus past her house. He rode his bike down her street. He went to the movies and bought an extra ticket for the not-her. It was somewhat overwhelming considering how busy he'd become with the Coalition—especially after Albert, Coalition president, had begun giving him additional responsibilities. By the time Mr. Hunter had been elected to an official office of the Coalition, he'd already absorbed a number of new people into his Jenna routine—carving out old places for where they weren't in his life. What had started as a simple gesture soon became a complicated ritual that took up most of his day. Sarah and Gail and Anne and Thomas and Allen and Emily and Jessica and Ellen and Gail and Ellen and Anne and Emily and Gail all kind of molded into Jenna, and Mr. Hunter had to ride past houses and make phone calls and buy presents and leave messages and write letters and open doors and run errands for her all while running much of the Coalition. It exhausted him.

8

Having been granted more power and leverage, he took it upon himself to start adding ideas to public work designs, ideas that might make his daily ritual a little simpler: a new side street here, a few more emergency exits there, a parking lot between this and that, bike lanes, etc., all in order to help him have enough time to not do things with people who weren't there. He even managed to pass some legislation leveling an entire block on the south side, the first in a long list of larger and more daring adjustments. Just as the city had once taken the physical form of everyone's knowledge of the former presence of the goats, it now took on the physical form of Jenna's absence in Mr. Hunter's life, and a growing list of people he no longer had time for. Streets conformed to where they weren't and made room for what they wouldn't do.

The city became increasingly difficult to navigate because other projects competed with Mr. Hunter's. And it became equally hard for him to hide his severe misuse of Coalition and taxpayer funds. By his tally, Mr. Hunter had at least fifteen employees unknowingly and exclusively building an immense network that traced Jenna's notness across the city, like a tuna net over a dolphin. It was only a matter of time before one of them started questioning what long bike rides around the green had to do with not-goatness. How many times could they be told that buying an extra movie ticket on Saturday afternoons had anything to do with reaffirming an absence of goats and celebrating the blessings of everyday not-goat-life before someone cracked it wide open? Mr. Hunter constructed alibis, but none of them were very realistic. He looked for loose ends, but oh, it was all loose ends.

9

Frankly, he just wasn't doing anything he was supposed to anymore. It was all not-Jenna, not not-goats, and so Mr. Hunter suspected suspicion all around him. One employee—a good employee, a great employee!—had begun asking knowing questions and dropping what Mr. Hunter believed were subtle hints. "Do you have any children, Mr. Hunter?" he'd asked, or "Sir, how are you feeling today? You look down, maybe you should go home and be with your family?" So what could he do? He fired the employee, Ericson Froemer, and directed him to take a new job Mr. Hunter'd "heard about" in a distant city. The spies were everywhere though: someone rifled through Mr. Hunter's blueprints and schematics, leaving them smudged and shuffled, so what was he supposed to do? Sit back and take it? He burned the whole filing cabinet in a trash can, along with some office furniture and a few desk trinkets, on the outside of town. He did what he could, but still the note arrived:

Mr. Hunter,

We need to talk. My office. Tomorrow afternoon.

Thanks,

Albert Cremacher
Coalition President

In a fit, Mr. Hunter burned more, items both from the office and his home—papers, miscellaneous memos, unread books, over-worn socks, and almost anything he could dare to part with that might tie him to his own wife. He stuffed any and all of her remaining belongings into closets and trunks and behind the couch and armchairs. He scrubbed his office twice. He bought new things, things unrelated to him or her or anyone really, and hung them around the office. To obscure the trail, he wrote notes about half-imagined projects, relating to no one or nothing in particular, and left voicemails about all manner of trivial things to everyone in his phone book. The evidence still stood, though, because he simply could not tear down the whole city, all of the places he had marked with not-Jenna's stink. And so he arrived at Albert's office the following afternoon with finger's crossed, hoping Albert might not see the trees for the forest, not-Jenna for the city.

"Sit down, Mr. Hunter," Albert said, an unmarked folder in his hands. Albert wore a suit and tie, unusual for a man most often seen in jeans or khakis, and he silently perused some documents. "First," he said, looking up suddenly and brushing back his hair, strangely combed and styled, "I have to say I'm really disappointed in you." Mr. Hunter made as if to speak but thought better of it. What could he possibly say in his own defense? "The fact of the matter is, you've been doing a lot of unsanctioned work around here, Mr. Hunter." He closed the folder and placed it on the desk. Someone rifled through my files, Mr. Hunter remembered. It must all be in there, every last bit. He had to say something.

"My wife," he started.

"Your wife? What does your wife have to do with this? Listen, we're all very sorry about your loss, I hope you know that, truly, but let's stay on track here." Confused, Mr. Hunter nodded. "I don't mean to be rude, but I'm going to level with you," Albert said. "If it were a different situation, I'd have to fire you. But the fact of the matter is, your self-initiated not-goat projects are really quite something. You skipped all the proper channels, and they seemed a little strange to us at first, but my god, have you done a bang-up job. The not-goatness of the city has really reached a new level because of you. The path around the park, the movie tickets, the city block—all of it really—it's brilliant. It took us a while to figure out that it was really coming from within the Coalition, from your department." He smiled briefly, then got serious. "We're an enterprise in the public eye, though, and the Coalition deserves some credit for the work of its employees, so I'm afraid I'm going to need full disclosure from you in the future. It's for the good of everyone really."

11

"Of course," Mr. Hunter agreed, trying to figure it all out.

"Great, then I'm sure you'll accept our offer of a promotion to Direct Intervention Specialist? You see, we've got a lot of new, uh, situations cropping up, and we think there's really no one better to handle them. You've got a keen eye, Mr. Hunter, really keen." Albert put out his hand. "Well, can we count on you?"

Dazed, Mr. Hunter agreed, shook hands, and in a flurry of back-claps and cheers and congratulations, found himself sitting in a brand new office with a fresh new cadre of underlings and a stack of projects spanning the whole city. His department had been given the task of working with a special set of clients and situations. What once had been thought of as a few curious but isolated incidents had suddenly ballooned into a storm of odd but similar requests. People all around the area wanted not just to be in a city that reminded them of the goats and where they weren't, but to put themselves back inside the terrible times they'd lived through, in order to re-experience the epidemic more fully. One woman, Mr. Hunter's first official client, whispered that even though the time of the goats had been traumatic and horrifying, it had also been liberating and opened up a new part of her that she was having trouble remembering. She missed, among other things, the itchy hairs sticking to the corners of her mouth and tickling her nose. And other clients reminisced, eyes askance, about the way this or that had been chewed, about the garbage being overturned, about the impediment to traffic, not to mention the idle days and slow, uncertain evenings.

Each request called for obvious solutions, but Mr. Hunter hesitated to implement them. He had been promoted based on his work not-Jennafying the city—could he really abandon that now? Besides the fact that he'd be turning his back on his wife, might it also expose him by exacerbating the distinctions between his not-Jenna work and not-goat work? He had no choice really, he felt, and opted just to use the same methods he'd used all along. With some of this and a little of that, he carved people's homes and neighborhoods into even finer shrines to what his wife wasn't. And again it worked: "It's even better than I had imagined," one person said, pointing to what, in Mr. Hunter's eyes, represented an elementary school music pageant that his wife had once taken a bit part in. "I can feel it," she said. They all loved his work and over the next few years of progress, it engulfed almost the whole city. He did volunteer work too: he helped community organizations fight real estate companies bent on buying up land without neighborhood input, to help protect historic buildings. Thus, though he regularly transformed the city, he also helped to preserve much of it, so long as it served his own purposes. He only lost one preservation case, the sugar factory, which was leveled and turned into a complex of chain stores and a mega-gym overlooking the shore. People were angry and sad at the defeat, but one loss is pretty good, he thought.

No surprise then that he became a sought after figure and in time was asked to do some extra work in another

13

part of the country. Albert flew him out to do the job, for which the Coalition would be paid kindly, and allotted a few extra hotel nights for Mr. Hunter to relax a bit before his appointment with the mayor. "You deserve it," Albert said. And maybe he did, Mr. Hunter thought, why not. After the flight, he checked in at the hotel and had a drink at the bar attached to the lobby. Gazing out the window to the streets, Mr. Hunter studied some of the buildings. The people here had done some interesting not-goat work, too, he thought, though it left him a little uneasy somehow. Through the door to the lobby, he caught a glimpse of a woman: short blond hair, ripped jeans, a large backpack. He saw her face only for a second, but registered it immediately—Jenna. He awkwardly dropped some money, too much or too little, on the bar and ran after her through a maze of other guests checking in or out, but she stepped into a cab before he could catch her. In the lobby, he demanded information about the woman, but the portly attendant outright refused "to betray the confidence of any guest at this hotel." The only things he'd give up were that she had not checked out, just left for the evening, and he agreed as well to take a message for her, a note asking her to meet Mr. Hunter at the bar, where he would be waiting until she got back.

It was almost two in the morning when she sat down next to him. "Do I know you?" she asked. Mr. Hunter, turned to see her, and oh, she was beautiful, eyes heavy with untold experience, her face and mouth mature and wise, so many stories to tell, yes, all of that, but no, she was not Jenna—not even not-Jenna, but just some woman who had nothing to do with who his wife was or wasn't.

"No," he said. "I'm sorry. I thought you were someone else." She left, a little confused, and Mr. Hunter stepped out for some air. Over the course of the next few days, he attempted to relax and enjoy himself, but his Jenna encounters continued. He kept almost spotting her: an ugly woman working behind the counter of a pharmacy, an elderly man in a long coat walking his dog, a collection of crossed shadows raised against wood paneling, an assortment of knickknacks tossed onto a waiting room table, a smell lingering outside a utility closet, but nothing came together as her because it all was something else entirely.

15

While riding the elevated train line across the city, out of boredom or desperation or chance, Mr. Hunter stumbled upon what should have been so obvious to him before. In the curve of the tracks, he felt something familiar. The way it arched around this building and brought the cars in line with an angular vista of parking lots and piping, the way traffic flowed beneath the rails and spilled into a newly drawn intersection, it all added up; he had been seeing Jenna, or perhaps more precisely not-her. He had to get off at the next stop and check some math, observe a few streets, and thumb through his notes in order to confirm it, but, yes, these were his plans, all around him, his designs. The city had been restructured with his memories in mind, albeit a bit shabbily. All the hallmarks of the urban not-Jenna he had built at home were etched throughout the corners and bike lanes and gutters and trusses, but as far as he could remember he had never been to this city before. He took a seat on the sidewalk and, for the first time, considered the fact that he might be losing it a little. Perhaps this epiphany, he thought, is the one that really should have been so obvious to him all along.

The question of his mind's well-being kept him distracted and slightly short of breath the next day as he met with city officials, ugly men who belabored points with boring and farcical details about zoning and property lines. Their good impression of Mr. Hunter no doubt dwindled as they talked expressively over coffee and crumb cakes in a carpeted conference room downtown. Mr. Hunter hadn't been able to pull a clean outfit together that morning let alone himself, and he was only barely in the room. The mayor's bald head became an unintended focus, where Mr. Hunter stared and mulled over his own sanity, questioning its strength or even existence amid the absurd blather of numbers and figures and projections, leaving the mayor outwardly uncomfortable under Mr. Hunter's constant gaze. The hairless spot glistened and shined softly above the few thin slices of wispy brown hair closely cropped along the mayor's temples, and it had Mr. Hunter's complete attention when an aid mentioned "our sadness at the loss of our former urban planner, a Mr. Ericson Froemer, really quite a talent."

"Who?" Mr. Hunter asked.

"Ericson Froemer," the aid repeated. Someone rifled through my files, Mr. Hunter remembered. He looked out the window at the city skyline: it must all be in there, every last bit. Alert, Mr. Hunter asked Mr. Froemer's whereabouts, but the city officials had no real record or information. He'd simply left without coming into work one day, "about a year and a half ago," they said, "we've basically just been floundering since then, which is why we were so excited to invite you, but we still have some thinking to do, of course, with the budget cuts and all, so you'll understand if," but Mr. Hunter didn't even stay to listen. He was out of his chair, out the door and into town records within fifteen minutes, at Froemer's old apartment in another twenty, boarding a plane with a forwarding address from the landlord in just under two hours, and landing in a new city in four.

It was the same thing all over again. The streets, the paths, the routes and the alleys; the wiring, pipes, ducts and chutes; the rampways, doors, landings and vestibules—all of it just more not-Jenna scribbled on a new landscape. Who the hell did Froemer think he was, Mr. Hunter thought, and what did he want with his not-wife? An inquiry at the town hall turned up nothing but a lead on another city, and so it continued in one city after another: Mr. Hunter found less and less of his wife and even less of Froemer. The notness of Jenna in some ways began to mold with the notness of the rogue urban planner, and the new and many structural iterations of Mr. Hunter's stolen plans became increasingly complex across the country, as if Froemer had begun taking absurd and unprecedented liberties. Some cities, despite ultimately staying true to the basic blueprints Mr. Hunter had devised at home, were more like thick metal webs of memory, rusted steel girders emblazoning all the subtle lines he'd envisioned. Froemer was butchering Mr. Hunter's past with melodrama and gaudy flourishes, spitting all over what Jenna wasn't wasn't and never would or could be.

Months passed before Mr. Hunter finally caught up with him. In the center of a small town in the northwest, Froemer kept an office right above a well-established laundromat and dry cleaning service. Ignoring the absurd ways in which streets and corners channeled his wife, Mr. Hunter marched right in to see him. A secretary said he'd stepped out to a meeting about an hour earlier, but that he'd "be back soon if you wanted to leave a message." After some arguing, the wiry man let Mr. Hunter wait in the lobby with him while he secretaried, so long as Mr. Hunter kept quiet and didn't touch anything. The walls were bare of adornment but smudged with some kind of film or grease. Half opened boxes lined the baseboards, ready to be further unpacked or repacked at any moment, whatever the need may be. Froemer was either running from or chasing something, but he had an unmistakably casual air when he stepped through the door in his tweed suit. His secretary attempted to introduce him, but Froemer wouldn't have it.

"Mr. Hunter!" he said, as if he'd expected him. "God, there's a lot to talk about, isn't there?" He smiled, taking off his jacket, and added, "Let me make you a drink," gesturing to his office. Mr. Hunter followed him, took off his hat, and had a seat while Froemer scrounged through some boxes for some rocks glasses and a bottle of gin. "I'm glad you made it out here," Froemer said. He had a mini-fridge behind his desk or worktable or card table from which he grabbed some ice and tonic and lime. On the wall hung a poster with a picture of an excised tumor, beneath it emblazoned the word *PROGRESS* and Froemer's company logo. What the hell did that mean, Mr. Hunter wondered. Did it suggest progress to be a cancer? Or that removing cancer equaled progress? He took a breath and looked around. Very few things were unpacked, or most things were already packed, Mr. Hunter couldn't tell, but a number of photographs were tossed about the room. "I won't ask how you found me, of course, as it's a blessing I'm here at all, and I have only you to thank," he said with some hesitation. Frames sat with their backs to Mr. Hunter so that he could not see what pictures they contained. In fact, Mr. Hunter realized, as Froemer handed him his drink, there were a few boxes with more photo albums jutting out all around the room. Humidity thickened the air—Mr. Hunter felt that he could push his hands right through the furniture as if through oatmeal or grits or meat. "I've heard that you've made a name for yourself outside of The Coalition, too," Froemer said, and Mr. Hunter recognized something in the way he glanced at the pictures in front of him, only a brief look, a darting of the eyes, but also a twitch of the cheeks, a softening of the mouth. Within half a second, Froemer was back to his casual self, as if it hadn't even happened, but still Mr. Hunter had seen it. A warmth, a longing.

Jenna.

Mr. Hunter stood up with his drink and paced the room

19

so that he could get a better view of the frames. "Are you all right?" Froemer asked. Mr. Hunter turned, sipping at his gin, and examined Froemer's face. He looked good, fresh, happy. Froemer smiled, his mouth wavering with a few subtle shakes between expectant, malicious, and stupid. Mr. Hunter stepped back slowly, waiting for the frames to show their face, and said nothing to Froemer. The man had taken his notes, he thought, all of his blueprints and plans—could he have stolen his wife, too? Was she here somewhere? No, that wasn't possible, he thought, but maybe Froemer had slept with her while she was in The Coalition so long ago, and here in these frames would be the history he'd never seen, the real things she had done all those late nights that she spent working for "the cause." Was Froemer's perversion of his blueprints actually more accurate, based on an intimacy Mr. Hunter had never known? When he felt his back hit the wall, standing in the corner of the room near the window, Mr. Hunter could make them out, photo after photo: birds. Or, more precisely, many pictures of one bird. He couldn't fathom it: not Jenna or not-Jenna, but a bird? Within the boxes, some photos were exposed as well, more of the blank-faced thing: Froemer with the bird, a woman with the bird, the bird and some trees, the bird and a young boy, old pictures, new pictures, cheap pictures and large portraits, a whole life peppered with this animal. "You'll excuse the mess I hope," Froemer said.

"Is this your, uh...bird here?" Mr. Hunter asked.

"Oh, ha, yeah...had him all through high school and college, yep, but he...well, he died a few years back. Birds do sometimes." He drank his gin and went on, "Why do you ask?" Froemer smiled only slightly. And just for a moment, there was that look again.

Mr. Hunter took his gin and tonic in one gulp and then demanded another. "You, too," he said, "pour yourself one, too."

"What?"

"This is how we do it," Mr. Hunter said. "This is it."

"Do what?"

Mr. Hunter hadn't the slightest idea what he intended, but still sputtered out, "Shutup and drink, kid."

Confused, yet somehow drawn in, Froemer poured out two more glasses, the heat of competition sparking within him. Locking eyes, the men threw back their drinks as if hitting golf balls toward a distant green, and, wiping his mouth, Froemer knew enough to pour another. Something—or nothing—was at stake. What was or wasn't it? They aimed to find out.

They drank all night, speaking only with their eyes, eyes alternately betraying animosity and revealing common warmth. Each imagined stuffing the other into a box and mailing it to the past or future—who knew which? did it matter?—and both waited patiently for the opportunity to slip quietly into the walls, their blood joining the wires and planks if only to outdo the other. But instead, they simply passed out, neither of them winning or losing the game—because they never established the rules, only the procedures.

Mr. Hunter woke early and in need of water. Froemer

was asleep at his desk, snoring. Amber and white light exposed a line of dust making its way to nowhere, dead skin mixing with the assorted fragments and debris of the building. Outside the office, Froemer's secretary had just arrived to start the day. With a wave, Mr. Hunter and the secretary shared a confused glance while he let himself out. Straight away, he headed for the airport but hesitated in the lobby, watching people come and go. He took the last flight home and, high over the country through the evening and into the night, saw the lights coming on in the darkness and imagined a tumor, or whatever it was, spreading or receding with each new wire strung bright along the road, one idea becoming the other.

He arrived just after dawn and took a slow walk through the streets as shops opened up and owners dusted off the sidewalks; there were still no goats, no Jenna, no nothing, all just as he had built it. A crowd of picketers gathered near the town center, a community organization taking on the encroaching real estate companies. They stood in the early morning air, their breath visible against colorful wool hats, agitated and determined. Mr. Hunter figured now was the time to get back into the flow of things, step back into routine, and he asked a thirty-something man, somewhat thick around the middle, what the cause was. He told Mr. Hunter that the town preservation committee had been "fighting to keep The Complex alive" as he shook hands with arriving picketers. "We'd love to have your help. This complex of stores brings business to town," he said, "and that mega-gym is a staple of our community. What are they going to do with this space? It doesn't matter because," here, he yelled, "*we like it the way it is!*" He paused, "Right?" And some nearby picketers cheered. Through the crisscrossing of buildings and trees and cars and his memories, Mr. Hunter could see the area where the sugar factory used to stand, the one they had fought for and lost. What was at stake here? The people didn't want to replace these events with new events anymore, but to replace them with the same events, Mr. Hunter thought. If we could only keep it the same so much longer, we'd make the end the same as the beginning, but not a rose is not a rose is not a wife is not a bird is not a gym is not a goat is not anything is not, Mr. Hunter thought, and it just keeps going.

23

EUCLID'S POSTULATES

1. A straight line segment can be drawn joining any two points.

"Nothing works until it does," the mechanic says, but my Mazda remains indifferent to such wisdom, stubborn on the side of the highway. It's 6am and I could use something sweet.

"Chetty D" rubs a rag over greased palms and gazes at the sedan, stumped. "Damn, that's a real pickle." Across the state, Nithya texts incessantly at me for not arriving or calling. I consider the distance between exits, always getting longer. Miles of nothingness. No matter where I am now, I should be able to get where I'm going, I think, if only because I am in love, but the Mazda overlooks this too.

Chet waddles along the dirt-worn shoulder to his battered tow truck. Does he think I'm Muslim? He probably thinks I'm Muslim. Chet grabs some flaccid rubber wand with one hand and a curved pole in another, then smiles, waving the obscure items at me as if both their disparate utilities and the logic connecting them should be obvious. He's giddy, and I smile too, thinking: Chetty D's clinched it, thank god, I will make it to the funeral after all.

Chet dives into the gears, then squirms wormlike and ever more snugly into the folds of metal. A hero. He enters the machine so thoroughly, in fact, that I wonder if his plan hinges merely on imbuing this engine with his whole pear-shaped body, finally sacrificing himself to my car in a merger of professional purity: The Perfect Mechanic. That I've approached my sex life in an analogous fashion dawns on me now and I am privately embarrassed. I hear a wrenching. Maturity comes, not gradually with experience, but in sudden bursts of rarified shame. A clinking. Nithya's mother is dead, and I am drafting a plan to better disguise my perverse egoism as humanity. Scraping. Examining my sleeves, I try to forget that I have lived not only this particular life but any life at all. It doesn't work. Silence. Chet's form slackens, save for a final tension deep in his shoulders. He emerges from the engine with a smirk as if grasping some clever joke's elusive punch line, then pivots around the hood and into the driver's seat. "So, are you a Muslim?" he asks. "No, Catholic," I say. "My parents are from India." Turning the key, he listens and waits. I, too, listen and wait.

The highway offers nothing but the twang of distant industry. The ground is damp. I envision the rubbery knob flopping into position along the curved pole, finally reviving the blanked engine via symmetry. I believe in an unknown narrative binding their purpose beneath the hood. Instead, a terrible wheezing begins from the engine. Will it ever stop? I don't think Chet's plan has worked.

Stuttering, the engine sounds as if it has learned miraculously to breathe, and as such, also to suffocate. I swear that one of us, either this mechanic or myself or the car, will cry. No tears drop, though a face does burst into flames. Undeniably, the hood of my Mazda is on fire. The hood of my Mazda is on fire. Chet scrambles away. My car has maybe exploded?

The phone rings. Nithya. I don't answer. In a ball of fire, 'maybe' is consumed. I cannot drive a flaming car to a funeral, I think. Nor an explosion of any kind. Ill-advised. A tire pops. Something shoots across the jersey barrier. To see it all before me, flames roaring into the sky, I cannot help but wonder at the awesome power of anything becoming something else. Is it always so miraculous? Chet manages, thank god, to put it out, then joins me to stare at the smoke. "Maybe everything works until it doesn't," he says. I could use something sweet.

2. Any straight line segment can be extended indefinitely in a straight line.

"What?" Nithya says on the phone. I steal anxious

glances through Chet's rearview, half expecting the Mazda dragging behind us to implode, but it just bobs gently in rhythm with the road. My car will not be attending the funeral. It's dead.

The situation provides ample room for optimism, I tell Nithya. With church services scheduled three hours off, there's time still to rent a car and make the two-hour drive. Calm and understanding, she agrees almost offhand. Grief is different for everyone. Her tone is bland to the point of absurdity in the face of her mother's death, or any death. Nithya speaks as through a cloth around her mouth, a gauzy linen drawn about her life. She tells me about her knees, about the baked ziti, potpourri, some lamb shank, peas, children. Out of respect or empathy or social etiquette, I stuff that gauze in my mouth too. How can I tell you anything, I think, even car rentals. In a sea of barely real exchange, the actual always looks the clown, until—faced with the clown itself— our ostentation becomes ridiculous. Death's balloon animals. I am in love, mothers die, cars explode, and we speak quietly over the telephone. When the circus leaves town, there is no town. The truck jolts, my phone falls to the floor.

First it's just bumpy, then more than that. The vehicle seizes up, violently retching. I am slammed against the window as Chet rams the hulk off the road into the dirt. The hood smokes. "Damn," he says. "How about that."

Yes, how about that. Is my car poisonous? Contagious? No matter, we are here, stranded. Chet laughs, makes a call. I laugh too. Nithya, when I tell her, reacts like I explained the weather, cares only that I'll eventually arrive. Chet assures me, and I picture Nithya in the house, floating like dander or ghosts.

A larger truck arrives. Two unruly men hook it to Chet's, pull theirs forward into the expanse. They spin wheels into the mud—so deep in fact that the large truck cannot drive or go or move. And neither can we, or the Mazda, or anything at all. Everything is here, by the highway, in the mud. We are stuck. Ha. Making it to the funeral, at least on time, is starting to seem unlikely. I laugh, sort of. Also, are we cursed?

Ten minutes later, another truck arrives. Impossibly, a bust. Then another. I am uneasy. In less than an hour, we're four tow trucks deeper and no closer to movement. Just further into the dirt. I do not tell Nithya this, or that my car is a plague, always has been.

Chet, exasperated hero, calls his wife. She will drive me to the rental spot, but I feel guilty inviting another party into our improbable scenario—do we have a responsibility to warn them off? Careful, Don't touch, Our lives are contaminated. The pattern of collapse cannot be contained. I can see a line of doom emanating from my vehicle, crossing the Cartesian plane of this town, saying: You will survive, *but your car will not*.

While I wait, numerous mechanics pace and loiter. Confederate flags abound. I make bets with myself about which portion of these men assumes I'm Mexican, as opposed to that which assumes I deserve this exploded car, or resents me for having caused so much havoc, now or ever. 90/50/10,

29

maybe? One mechanic rests against his bumper, examining a notebook and gesticulating. He is young, peach-fuzzy. "There exists such a point T," he says, "and there exists such a line L," he jerks, "that line L intersects segment D and," but he trails off. He starts again, waving at the sky. This is not merely late-semester cramming. Theater maybe? I assume he must be explaining ideas to a student via phone, because he keeps pausing mid-thought, as if interrupted, but there is no earpiece, and the thoughts themselves are not wholly correct or worthy of teaching, and not so much interrupted as incomplete: half-baked ramblings clawing at ideas that are not there. "Sorry if I'm driving you crazy," he says, noting my interest, eyes like nails, "but I have to do this aloud...because nobody knows the shape of space. Not me. Not you." Uh-oh.

"No problem at all," I say. He continues, diagramming the air. I'm afraid he'll snare me into some pointless conversation. I can't help but assume the words are merely decorative here, festooning the empty belief that a narrative ripples beneath the facts. Something about space, about shape, about us. He twitches, blinks, smacks his lips. Why is math so attractive to the vaguely schizophrenic? Why do we want so badly to dredge stories out of symmetries? To see correlations between people and things, often unfounded, and to wrap fiction around disparate bodies? Am I Muslim. The mere feeling of a pattern, the suggestion of one, can be as seductive as patterns themselves, I think, and note my complicity in this. Obviously, the rescue squads en route to our breakdown are not and have never been doomed from the start by a line drawn outward from my Mazda and its plight, and no underlying system of failure has threaded its way from my car to the tow trucks and beyond, nor is said line waiting patiently to embroil the nearest bystander. The pattern and its narrative is me, where it begins and ends, not the fire or the road.

Time bears this out. Soon, I am in Chet's wife's car, and I am waiving goodbye, and I am at the rental place, and I am filling out insurance forms, and I am driving off to a funeral, safe and steady, and to Nithya, and her mother, entirely uncursed, though I can't shake the feeling that I have not escaped that pattern of breakdown and collapse, which does not exist, and that I have not broken off from that line of failure, which isn't there, but that I am now simply dragging it along behind me, stretching it to capacity, hauling it straight to everyone I love.

3. Given any straight line segment, a circle can be drawn having the segment as radius and one endpoint as center.

Ha! Freedom! The open road! My arm out the window! The rental car smells fantastic: clean, fresh and safe. Like summer towels. Like fruit. Like home. Yes, this rental car is my house, I think, my bed. I gun down the highway, into the mouth of the future. It's 9am. I will be late, yes, but I will arrive at the funeral. I am alive and the road flies out behind me. See you in two hours, Nithya. I am in love and the earth turns around my rental car. It's 9am. Everything is in motion and fluid and responsive. I remember this feeling from when

I was a kid, a smiling idiot imitating an action hero, swinging my arms and legs, making the weakest of sound effects: *fwoosh, wham, kathoosh*. I am that motion, that sound, and so is the road.

Do I still suspect highway curses? Yes, but I'm dismissing that! It's easy. Look: I press the gas and I go. I press the brakes, I slow. I'm on my way—the world is as it should be. Crisis averted.

Now, though, I am tasked with the unfortunate responsibility of explaining to Nithya that I will be late. In my mind, Nithya is all hair, tossing, turning, coming to rest. A gentle breeze carries me away. I can't conceive her body without also conceding her laugh, the best of all. And I must tell her I'll be late. To her mother's funeral. That I will not help prepare her, will not carry her safely from warm ambiguity to cold certainty, cannot provide a net of comfort as she falls into this world, but instead will walk in mid-service, alone, a stranger, the door creaking, the heads turning, the world ending. But she will understand: *circumstances beyond our control*. What better time to invoke this reasoning than now, in that period surrounding death? Here, the impossible is revealed not only to be probable, but instead the only fact at all. Action, reaction. Death and/or Car Trouble. Imagine it: I turn the wheel, the car adjusts. I can do anything.

For example, I turn on the radio, and a pundit speaks. My body hurdles toward responsibility, mourning. I exit the highway, and the scenery changes. I am free. I stop the car, and the world stops with it. Real freedom must be measured, I think, only against that which we are *expected* to do. I look out of the car and—*poof*—I see a diner among the pines. And it must be measured by the degree to which we can deviate from that expectation without incurring costs, either financial or spiritual. I enter this diner and—*bam*—I am greeted. My body fills with lust and sadness. I sit down—*fwoosh*—I eat pie. Only when we commit wrongs are we free. More coffee please. I don't cry, though I could, and a weight is lowered on a string from my throat to my bowels. I am a coward. It's 10am, Nithya, I say, trembling in the booth with my flaky crust, and you will not believe the situation with my car, incredible.

But of course she believes it. How could she not. Who would lie about this. About any of this. How can I tell you anything, I think, even car rentals. I do not go to the funeral and—*kathoosh*—I do not go to the funeral. Nothing happens. *Wham.* Nothing happens. Not even a breeze.

4. All right angles are congruent.

By now, services are in full swing, and I've already eaten pie. What else is there. Frankly, I feel like an asshole (*fuck oh fuck, what have I done, Nithya shit shit, your mother*, etc., etc.), but I've already crossed the line of indecency. Time is irrevocable. In this, I recognize my transgression's implication that I have fun, that to have anything less than The Most Fun, in tandem with the funeral I'm missing, would be a desecration. We are so rarely afforded time in our lives. To waste it is an insult. I must act. Now more than ever.

Waitress, clear my plate.

33

Outside, I soak up the town. A strip mall parking lot. The sun glints, wind rustles. Something is half off. Something is buy-one-get-one. Where is my adventure? The dollar store? Shoe Mania?

I enter the arcade. I play games. I waste quarters, dollars. I defeat the sea monster, the robot encampment. Hymnals ring throughout the chamber. I strut about the supermarket. I stalk the pharmacy. Somewhere, Nithya's mother is paraded along pews, onlookers tethered to her inertia. I feel the weight of this fact on my heart and body, yet I rack up reward points via my CVS Club Card. I stand on the corner of two streets and don't move. I consider a bench but don't sit.

I inquire with a store manager about mountain bikes. I enter a scam contest offering two week cruises in the Caribbean, sponsored by a bogus home security outfit. Nithya must be inconsolable, which I both sense and cannot shake, while I see a movie with exorbitant CGI. I am at the center of the Earth, deep under rock. Outside in the parking lot, a family lopes across the asphalt. I balance on one leg. Nithya texts me that her own mother is really gone, is in the ground.

I have not only missed the services and burial, but I'm also not headed home for the reception, for the potpourri or baked ziti. I know too that I won't return for the whole evening, at least until morning, that I have found this balance between choosing to do something and allowing my choices to happen to me.

I am decided, though I can't say why. Because I entered a hollow of this earth where I feel safe and alone? No: in a gas station bathroom, I burst into tears. Only briefly. Then I giggle, kind of wildly, kind of forced. I shake my hips and smush my face. Someone knocks on the bathroom door, and I am afraid. I feel as if I've been discovered at the scene of the crime, that I am the body and the knife, and that it's all so mundane. Ha! What am I doing? I'm not drunk or gambling, and I am not with another woman or engaged in any crime. I'm just quietly walking around this town, but I am here, doing this, this thing that cannot be good, which is nothing in particular. "Just a minute," I say. What will happen in a minute? Nothing. There can be no positive course of action. Every decision, even the most banal, is a travesty. I flush nothing. I have the feeling that I've woken up in this moment without ever having lived before, that my whole life has appeared suddenly before and around me in a bathroom stall, like a burst of light at the edge of a field. Like a sound.

35

After buying a donut, I hover in a half-wooded area behind the gas station, and Nithya says she has so much hurt that she cannot contain it. Her voice wobbles like a fawn. I place my head against the bark of a wet tree, smell the sap, and I tell her I want nothing more than to be there, to hold her, and this is true, or not at all, but still true, and I stand in a patch of pines and I do not move, though I can, and I tell Nithya I'll have to spend the night here, though I needn't, because the rental car, because the insurance claims, because the backlog, because whatever. I pull that gauze from my mouth and weep but there is only more gauze, my whole mouth and throat and body.

She understands.

In a motel, I watch *Law & Order* and sleep.

Early in the morning, I return to Nithya in my rental car.

When we embrace on the lawn, it's 9:30am, and I wait to feel terrible, to really feel it, but it doesn't come. I anticipate Nithya's despair at my actions, but she only holds me a little longer, because yesterday has not actually happened, is nothing, because there are no elements that can evidence its occurrence, because it is a fiction beneath the facts (but what facts), a narrative that cannot be diffused across symmetries (but what symmetries), an unreachable conclusion on the other side of a graph (but what graph), and Nithya even if you suspect me (of what), you will say nothing, because you can only point me out to yourself or to others at the risk of sounding absurd or indelicate, because there exists a set of numbers that cannot be pronounced or counted, that has no sums.

Nithya, I am impossible and you are a hick that grasps at me in a field. Yes, I am getting closer to knowing what it means when I say I am in love.

5. If two lines are drawn which intersect a third in such a way that the sum of the inner angles on one side is less than two right angles, then the two lines inevitably must intersect each other on that side if extended far enough. This is analogous to what is known as The Parallel Postulate.

I think I'll get another drink from the lower deck bar— can I get you anything?

No, no, thanks—I'm all right. Had enough.

Good on you, darling! Don't wanna get seasick I take it—er?

Ha, I'm Nithya. So nice to meet you, again. A pleasure. I love your bathing suit.

Likewise, I'm Erica, but don't hesitate to ask again, Nithya. And that's your, uh, your husband there?

Yes, the little booby.

Is he sleeping?

Ha! I'd say so. Honey? Honey? What a little boob.

It must be all this sun, it's exhausting.

I know! And honestly, I mean, we're pretty emotionally drained, too. My mother passed just a few weeks ago, and so this vacation is both exactly what we need right now and sort of too much to handle, you know all at the same time, Jesus, and oh wow wow—that was maybe, maybe too much? I'm sorry, er, Erica. You're on vacation.

No, no, it's—it's okay. I'm so sorry to hear that, Nithya. Really. My husband's father died just last year. Indescribable. So sorry.

Yeah, I'm, ha, I'm, you know I can't say I'm really used to it, but all this sun is nothing to scoff at, right? And the ocean? And this guy, this lug, my husband, the poor thing, little boob, he couldn't make the funeral, he got into a car accident, if you can believe it, and the darn insurance wouldn't cover it at first, the jerks, and he was stuck in some town in the sticks, with some real characters, and oh it was just a mess, we all felt so bad for him.

37

Oh lord, yeah.

But then, you know, we won this cruise, out of the blue, just like that, which is maybe bad timing, or not, and anyway it's, I mean it's so surreal to be here and all, with this weight and you know all this space and, uh, heaviness, but good too, really really good. I don't know. I mean, sometimes nice things happen. Nice things can be painful. The ocean is really sobering.

Yeah. Do you swim?

Do I swim? Sure, I love it. Try to get—hey, look at that.

What?

There, out there, you see?

Oh wow, yeah, yeah, that's what? Like, another ship?

I think so.

So strange to see it here. There. So sudden. Where'd it come from?

I know. I'd gotten used to all this water and sky and emptiness, just floating out here alone. Or—not alone, ha, there's got to be, what, a few thousand people on here, more maybe, but you know, like out in the ocean. That kind of alone, just this cruise liner in the water in the dark, miles of nothingness all around us.

And now this new thing, out there, so close, yeah.

What's it doing there? Is it, wait, is it real?

I feel like I'm looking at a whale or something, but it's just people.

Is that fire?

No, that's like fun or excitement, I think. Lights.

Where did it come from? Is it getting closer?

What do you think is happening over there?

Drinking? Gambling? Screwing? Same things we're doing.

Yeah, but maybe it's a different kind of ship.

Is there another kind of ship?

What do you mean, *Is there another kind of ship?*

That's it. Is there another kind of ship. Is there another kind of ship.

Wait, like what, like besides a cruise liner?

Yeah, I mean, yeah. Just—is there another kind of ship. Or anything really. You know? Does that make sense? Is there another kind of ship, or anything. God, wait, hahaha, Jesus, what's wrong with me, Erica? Brain fart. I mean: is it going where we're going? That ship, will it stay there like that in the water with us the whole time? I mean, where else can it be going now that it's here? Where else can you go from this spot in the ocean once you're here? Are you awake, honey—look at the ship.

39

INTERIOR DESIGN

"Listen," Karen says, "it'll be our place. Not yours or mine, but ours, and the furniture should be right."

For once, I concur. Decor more than fills space; it acts as mutual agreement, ongoing contract and statement of purpose. Coffee makers, beds, bureaus, paintings, clocks, and wine racks, beyond their utility, affirm the trust between people who choose to face those objects together again each day, to let things invade their lives anew every morning, in concert and without pause.

A little affirmation might go a long way, too, after our last few arguments. Most relationships don't last, and interior design remains so often ignored in the discussion of why and how. Feelings change faster than the objects around them—the right furniture can act as a trusted anchor tying us to the ideals we forget, standards we transgress and loves we abandon, drawing us back from our uncoiling humanity to the life we once promised we wanted.

Likewise, the wrong objects and arrangements can wedge themselves between us and who we think we are, driving a stake between now and the future. Materialism is not, as is the common understanding, a superficial fault, but instead the sum of all things. Love is the strongest force on Earth only when bolstered by the right array of throw pillows and duvets, the correct mixology of rugs and ottomans.

So, before we move, I throw out my old couch and the broken dresser, I put my grandmother's table in storage. Karen leaves her desk behind and tosses the stools. We move into the apartment hauling only eight garbage bags' worth of clothes, ten boxes of books, a bottle of whiskey and some mismatched plates.

The first night, we stand under the ceiling fan and stare across the expanse of floorboard, hold hands and laugh, run through the rooms and hide in the darkness amidst our own echo. Busy with work, we go days without buying or adding a single piece of furniture, then weeks. We return home each night to find that same unfilled space. It's fantastic and we are in love. We blast music from the tiny speakers on our phones, eat dinner off the floor and fall asleep heaped in each other's arms—in the corner, a doorway, a windowsill. The rooms are empty but for us and what we want from each other, which is everything and nothing all at once, though no one is making claims or accounting for debts. Our life is shapeless and undetermined. I lose weight. Karen smokes less. Sex abounds. We are garden sprinklers on a hot afternoon. Our days spray formlessly in all directions, and the bare walls catch us like paint on blank canvas.

Then the furniture comes.

First, a microwave: its effect is immediate, though uncertain. I wake at 3am, stumble from a room (the living room? the bedroom? we still don't know). Getting water, I see the appliance at the counter's edge, marring the pristine slice of marbled pressboard. I feel its gaze, its judgment, and my belly weighs on me, jutting over underwear. In a moment of weakness, I nuke leftover takeout, far too much. I consider Karen's legs, splayed naked in the darkness beyond a doorframe. My reverie is interrupted by a sneeze.

But whose sneeze?

"Karen?" I call. Her toes curl some, but no response. I swivel again toward the microwave, peer at it over my glass.

43

"Hello?" I whisper into the cup, too ashamed to raise my voice. "Microwave?"

In silence, I eat my burrito. Then comes the couch.

We place it in one room, then another. Where the red bulbous thing lands doesn't matter though. Like a slow and steady fire, it changes everything. I find Karen smoking on it when I return from work. This is a surprise—her job usually persists well into the evening. She takes long drags and reads from a magazine. The couch wraps around her body, hugging thighs and pushing against ribs. Karen observes me and smiles.

"Sit," she says, patting the fat cushion.

I do, and Karen tackles me within seconds, ripping at my shirt and pulling off my pants. We fuck like bricks falling from a third story walk-up. Things crack, dust flies, people scream. Within minutes, she comes four times and barely looks at me. Naked, out of breath, and gulping down water in the kitchen afterward, I find scratches on my chest and specks of cloth on my penis, little red fibers, some lint. The microwave does nothing, just watches me stare at my genitals like an idiot. I walk back to what has clearly become our living room, confused and beaten, then fall into Karen's arms. I barely know where I am. She smokes another cigarette and rubs her hand along the soft red couch. A gentle purring lulls me to sleep.

When I wake, Karen is in running clothes, about to head out. "You should think about exercise, too," she says before slipping on her headphones. She returns unannounced and continues to read on the couch. I order Chinese alone.

Besides a growing and unnamable distance between us, life moves forward. The furniture keeps coming and the apartment takes shape. Shoe caddy on the door, towel hooks in the bathroom, umbrella stand in the hall, coatrack by the closet. Friends visit, gifts are exchanged, dirt accumulates. Infrequent sex continues to be raucous, inhuman, and violent, but still pleasurable. The red fibers persist, sometimes in strings, otherwise in clumps. Though we purchase an ample bed, Karen sleeps frequently on the couch. We don't fight, just fizzle, and I accept that maybe love, as it matures, is like the sea to fish: eventually, you don't even know it's there. Which is fine, really, and to be expected, I think, as I heat up a plate of nachos and old pizza at 2am, mindlessly rubbing my cheek against the fridge, listening to Karen's writhing moans pulse from the living room.

The other day, I arrived home early to find her riding the couch like a horse amid candlelight. I'd never seen anything so erotic in my life.

"You have to accept the fact that Karen and the couch are not only fucking, but in love," the microwave says. Of course.

"Yes," I nod, dragging my food out of its face and into mine.

The next day, I take action. First, I pour over the technical specifications for the couch and read product reviews online, trying to discern what exactly makes the thing more desirable than me. I give up on this angle, though, conceding that the root of desire is personal and ultimately unknowable. And, besides that, I can't hold a candle to the list of perks and innovations built into this couch, a true marvel of domestic ingenuity and industrial design magic. The couch, I know in my heart, is better than me. This is confirmed, of course, when Karen announces bitterly that the couch is leaving us, that it has found another apartment, another woman. It's been good, the couch says, really, and wishes us luck before waddling awkwardly out the door.

Karen is devastated and spends her days prostrate in the living room, weeping and inconsolable. I too am sad, if not for the $400 couch then for her. Everything in this world is so short-lived, even our couch affairs. I touch her arm but Karen brushes me away, needs to be alone on the floor. Dejected, I

45

try to establish a relationship with any object in the house that will take me, but the microwave wants to remain platonic. The dresser needs space. The television is already involved. The ironing board says I'm too fat.

When I clear away the takeout containers and heave my naked body onto the coffee table, rubbing myself coyly along its length, I wonder what familiar ocean this anchor will finally draw me back to. I am moving my arms in great arcs through the air—as if I'm already swimming, as if I'm already at the bottom of that huge, empty ocean. And it feels just like nothing at all. Like I don't even know it's there.

As hard as I can, I am trying to imagine how wonderful it will be.

PLUNGE HEADLONG INTO THE ABYSS WITH GUNS BLAZING AND LEGS TANGLED

The abyss was found in October but not formally studied until the following spring. The retired widower who discovered it had tried to hide it because he used it to get free cable. Apparently, by continuously tossing in leftover food or old post cards, he received over 6,000 channels from the abyss, some of which don't even exist. Even though he tuned in to what later was revealed to be the actual voice of President Grover Cleveland, posthumously trying to contact the American public via channel 4375 about a clothing line franchise, as well as sixteen channels broadcasting apparently live feeds of major historical events, the old man primarily used the abyss to watch syndicated reruns of Wheel of Fortune.

"It's better when I watch it through the bottomless black fearvoid in all of our hearts than when I watch it on basic cable," he told scientists after being forcibly removed from his home, slated to be leveled hours later. "I think the old thing somehow makes the prizes more exotic. I don't know the physics of it really, but it feels 100% right when I say it out loud like this."

Trying it, scientists claimed that saying it out loud did in fact make it feel 100% correct, whereas previously it hadn't, but the tenuous theory has yet to be corroborated or disproven primarily because the formal research team brought into lead the investigation of the abyss lost its federal funding after a change in political climate. Before committing suicide, Senator Elison, R-NC, famously spoke to the House about a bill detailing forthcoming research grants: "Was America founded on the emptiness that pervades everything we do everyday all the time everywhere? Ladies and gentleman, not my America. I mean, am I wrong in saying it? In having a proud faith that the America I know and love was founded, or at least *more* founded, definitely at least more founded, if not totally founded, on special boots for digging? No, I am not wrong, I am right: Special boots for digging brought to us by TelCo, which I have proudly invested in, are more American than some immensely infinite hole. I urge you all today to vote with your hearts—but not the part that is clouded in darkness and meaninglessness. Use the other more American parts like the left ventricle or even the tricuspid."

The abyss was subsequently sold at federal auction to a startup investment firm intending to sit on the purchase while its value appreciated. "Our analysts," one spokesperson said at the time of purchase, "are reporting that the abyss only increases its emptiness and is everyday comprised of more and more nothing*er*-ness—a word coined to describe the severity of this new nothing that goes beyond all previous notions of nothing. To be quite honest, I don't really get all the math behind it, but really, in our viewpoint, it's not so much an abyss as it is what we around the office are calling a goldmine river—that is, a river flowing with many individual goldmines instead of water—insomuch as it's true that nothing and gold are interchangeable.

And according to our advanced business models? They are."

After filing for bankruptcy, Zed Exchanges, Ltd. donated the abyss to charity in an attempt at a one-time tax break. The recipient, Planned Parenthood, took offense to their receiving the donation, however, and quickly had their lawyers expunge the unwanted real estate, selling it at extremely low cost to a young entrepreneur by the name of Ted Aplansky—who boasted of plans to open a luxury spa and resort, aptly named *The Last Resort*, specializing in "religious" retreats. "For too long the atheists of America have waited for a Mecca to call their own," he made clear to the press, "and it goes without saying that the Atheist Mecca will provide the emptiness we've all come to expect in our own lives—only at a much higher intensity than you have ever experienced before—and, in addition, it will also come complete with a complimentary mudbath because, *hey, what else is there?* Certainly not anything to believe in if you think about it long enough so that it becomes true to you personally!

And remember: it's complimentary, not insultory!"

Killed by wolves, Ted never lived to see his project reach completion. Riddled with bad luck and bad press, the abyss remained untouched, unsold, unpraised, and almost entirely enveloped by the framework of an unfinished resort complex. After years of inactivity and disinterest, the abyss was reabsorbed into Montana state property during a manic rezoning campaign led by a newly elected governor. Prompted by the disappearances of pets, children, and indigenous wildlife, a police investigation suggested that the abyss was a danger to the local community. "All I'm saying is," Chief Rickman elucidated, "we have on our hands a pretty big hole. I'm also saying that, according to my sources, kids can fit in this hole—if they so choose. Now, you put two and two together and you get my point—is what I'm saying if you do the simple math here, folks." As it was within walking distance of the local elementary school, it was only a matter of weeks before the local PTA raised enough money to build a barbed wire fence around the abyss, in addition to enlisting a twenty-four hour security force.

And so it was that Wilson Bettertone became a security guard of the endless void inside all of us and all around us—though admittedly concentrated most densely here at his post in the fields of Tandahone, Montana.

Wilson recalls a famous quote by someone sometime somewhere, he can't quite remember who or when or where: "When you stare into the abyss, the abyss also stares into you." Having more than enough time to stare into it himself,

52

Wilson can and does say with authority that "it doesn't so much stare back as it more often gooses you when you aren't looking—kind of a pinch in the rear—but then also it's kind of only your mind. You really have to stand on the edge of the nothingness hole to understand the feeling, though. Still, calling it a hole isn't exactly right either. That is, it isn't a hole at all—it's nothing at all. And it's not the type of nothing where there's just a bunch of empty space, like a desert or something or a canyon—no, it's more like the kind where there isn't even any empty space in the spot where there isn't anything to begin with. I mean, you can't *see* it like you can see a hole. But you also can't not see it, either—it's right not there where it isn't, just as plain as the day. 'There's the abyss,' you'd say if you saw it. Though, like I said, you kind of have to not see it up close and personal to really see what I'm talking about here. Or not talking about, for that matter."

53

Wilson is thirty years old and unmarried. Women complain of him: "He talks too much. He starts saying something about dinner and then all the sudden, three months later, he's still talking and you're driving drunk in a corn field because you hate your parents."

On a typical day, Wilson shows up at work, sits at his booth doing, as he puts it, "next to nothing." Now, he likes to say "next to nothing" specifically because doing nothing "kind of loses its meaning when you're sitting next to the abyss—which is quite literally doing nothing. Or, perhaps more precisely, not doing something. You can't tell which really, I've tried. In fact, I usually try to tell the difference between doing nothing and not doing something every day before lunch. It's exhausting." Wilson is slightly cross-eyed.

For the most part, no one comes and no one goes. "I see the night shift guard when I come in and he heads home to his wife. Otherwise, it's usually just me." The kids don't come anymore, and the invisible fence keeps the dogs out. Occasionally, though, an old man or drunk shows up shouting obscenities and tries to hop into the abyss, "crying or smiling or both or neither—or one and then the other or all of them kind of mixed together so it looks more like constipation. Most of the time, their wives died or left them or don't love them or never met or married them in the first place."

54   The night guard at the nothinghole is a drunk, his name is Ted Bancouver, and—to his credit—more people know the former than the latter. Apparently, he falls asleep on the job: security cameras caught a homeless man hopping the fence unmolested, and on Ted's watch, then hurling himself naked into the endless nothing holding the mayor's baby and a bagful of staplers reported missing earlier that day. Ted had no explanation for this, so he was docked three weeks pay. In addition, he received a nasty phone call from the office supply store owner, Mr. McGombathe. As Ted tells it, "McGombathe used the word *truncate* in a fashion that was both threatening and very creative. He moonlights as a poet when he's not managing the store, but he writes mostly with his penis and not so much on paper as on women."

More importantly, though, it is because of the mayor-baby-homeless-man-stapler incident that Wilson received the following letter:

> *Mr. Bettertone,*
>
> *Due to the recent Mayor-Baby-Homeless-Man-Stapler incident, measures are being taken to prevent accidents at your post. A Protective Hole is to be constructed sometime in the near future just to the South East of the abyss in order to confuse would-be "hoppers." Your cooperation is appreciated.*
>
> *Thank You,*
>
> *The PTA of Tandahone*

Accompanying the letter was a shovel.

"At first, I was a little unsure of how to build a fake existential abyss," Wilson recalls. Over the course of two days, though, he managed to dig one—six feet wide and three feet deep. "I was pretty impressed with myself, to tell you the truth. Still, it wasn't complete until I added the sign—it's the icing on the cake." A piece of cardboard leaning on a rock reads: *PLUNGE HEADLONG INTO THE ABYSS WITH GUNS BLAZING AND LEGS TANGLED!* An arrow points down toward the ditch below, "just to make sure" Wilson says.

As most of the time no one comes and no one goes, the pretend endless nothingness sat almost useless for months. And then things—as they tend to do—changed.

Mrs. Frambrot killed her husband with a can of green beans to the head. Their marriage had been on the rocks for

55

years due to different work schedules and the tribulations of child rearing. Sex had become a childhood memory and dinner an almost religious routine, masochistic and depressing. Yet, after her husband's heart attack, they managed to find a sort of peace. They remembered "what it means to be naked, vulnerable. The rocks slid away and the ice melted and we held each other for the first time, one carrying the other to nowhere in particular without moving, without breathing or thinking, just holding." Reenacting their lives together, Mrs. Frambrot tossed the beans to her husband, just as she had the night she got pregnant for the first time, and her husband tried, smiling, to relive the same memory at the same time in the same place, but he was too slow, his arms too weak. The can knocked him off his feet and his head into the kitchen counter. "He died before he hit the ground," an EMT said.

She arrived at the abyss carrying an empty fifth of tequila at 9am on a Tuesday in May. Weighing over three hundred pounds, limber from her nakedness, and strong from her drunkenness, she barreled through the fence at what Wilson claims was "over fifty miles per hour." The fence went down and so did she—straight into the Protective Hole, screaming and wiggling. Once in the hole, she proceeded to roll around, eating dirt and beating her face, until she passed out in her own vomit. She sat there for almost two weeks, licking dew from rocks, until she abruptly got up and walked toward the highway. She was picked up two exits down and is now reportedly a salesclerk at a lamp store in western Pennsylvania.

Soon afterward, Mr. Fuller, an unmarried fourth grade teacher at the elementary school, woke up one morning missing a leg—no explanation. "It's not there anymore," Chief Rickman made clear, "and that's what's most important here really if you follow a certain train of thought." There was no sign of forced entry and no disturbance in the house other than the missing leg. "Sometimes," the Chief went on to say, "people steal limbs. You don't hear about it so much because you wouldn't really believe it if you did. I mean, do you believe it right now? When I'm telling you at this moment? Here at this time? I know I don't. It's ridiculous. But still it's true." After three weeks, the leg showed up in Mr. Fuller's mailbox, stuffed in haphazardly. Hanging around the ankle was a note that read: *SORRY, WRONG LEG.* It was only two days later that his other leg was stolen just before breakfast.

57

On the following Monday, drunk and giggling in his wheelchair, Mr. Fuller made his way across the field between the school and the abyss, a line of skipping, hopping fourth graders trailing behind him. Mr. Fuller brandished a large American flag on a pole in one hand and a prosthetic leg in another. "Heigh-ho!" he yelled as he approached the still broken fence of the nothingnessfearvoidhole. Wheeling about wildly, he began to toss children into the Protective Hole, screaming with each toss, "Sorry, wrong leg!" The hole filled up pretty quickly, only a few children managing to escape, and then Mr. Fuller tossed himself in as well. "I don't really guard things so much as I just watch bad things happen," Wilson noted. "As a guard, it makes me feel pretty impotent.

I mean, what can I do?" Behind him, Mr. Fuller dragged children by their feet into the hole as they attempted to claw their way up and out. "I don't even have a gun. Sure, I could yell and scream or say very forcefully, 'Stop that!' but that doesn't make things change so much, really." Wilson sipped his soda through a straw and continued, "It's pretty pointless. All of it. I mean, I only make $7.50 an hour." Perhaps out of duty, Wilson turned to the Protective Hole and said firmly, "Stop it!" No one did, of course. With a shrug, Wilson turned back to his soda. "That's the beauty of the Protective Hole, I guess. I know it's a lie, but it's a lie that helps people, right?" One by one, the children slipped away, leaving Mr. Fuller crying in the Protective Hole, pulling himself around on his belly and waving his flag. As the children escaped, however, they made a beeline for the real abyss—because it looked like a clever place to hide. And that's how the fourth grade class of Tandahone Elementary fell into the endless nothingness inside all of our souls.

In most any other town, this might have been the end of Jimmy, Allison, Stewart, José, Kristy, Donald, William, Cara, Brenda, Frank, Carl, Stacey, and Ed, but the PTA of Tandahone is a force of nature. "It is a constitutional right that our children are educated," demanded one parent. "Just because they now live in a bottomless hole that extends in all directions in time and space doesn't mean that they are to be denied the rights of any other child. By the very nature of this thing, they are in our school's jurisdiction." Another parent continued, "When I moved to my new house on Tall

Bush Lane, no one made a stink about my child going to school—but now that Jimmy lives in the endless abyss of fear and meaninglessness? Now he's not good enough to get an education? What country is this?" It was decided that a full time tutor would be dispatched into the abyss to educate the "relocated" students. A long rope was wrapped around a Ms. Anselar's waist, tied to a tree, and labeled *DO NOT SEVER: PROPERTY OF TANDAHONE BOARD OF EDUCATION*. With a quiet dignity and silent acceptance, the newly hired tutor screamed loudly while a "special committee" of PTA chairpeople forced her into the abyss.

"Mostly, it's something to trip over," Wilson said of the rope. "It's also made my job a little harder. I've got more responsibilities now. Like every other Friday? I have to throw in Ms. Anselar's salary. And every day I toss in the lunches that the kids' parents make. On Christmas? I'm going to have to toss all their presents in there. Which means—you guessed it—I'm not getting the day off. What's the use, right?" So when, on a Thursday afternoon, the abyss dragged the tree anchoring the rope up from the ground and into the gaping black maw, Wilson was relieved, assuming that the children were gone now and that his day-to-day work would simplify. However, his relief was exchanged for grief upon receipt of the following letter:

> *Dear Mr. Bettertone,*
>
> *As a hired guard in the pay of the Tandahone PTA, you are obligated under contract to protect the citizens*

59

from the deep and endless blackness that stalks our every waking hour of life on this earth. Thus far, your employment has been marked by a poor quality of service. Be that as it may, you will be given a satisfactory yearly review mark upon completion of a task in keeping with your responsibilities.

You are to enter the endless nothing and retrieve the lost citizens of Tandahone. Failure to comply will result in immediate termination.

Thank you for you cooperation,

The PTA of Tandahone

Accompanying the letter was a steel chain, an industrial-grade electric crank and pulley system, one enormous stone pillar, and a hand-crafted broadsword.

"I can't afford to not have this job right now. What's the use fighting it? Ya know what I mean here? Sure, I could just up and quit because I'm afraid of jumping into this black and unending meaninglessness, but I think I'd be doing that anyway if I quit. It's all the same thing really, but the way I see it? In one scenario, I've got a job and in the other, I don't—so you see, even though it's the same, it's also kind of different in an important way." And with that, he proceeded to maneuver with a forklift the giant stone pillar, twenty feet tall and ten feet around, into a hole in the ground. He wrapped the chain around it, threading it through the pulley system, and placed the sword in the dirt beneath.

He stood up, grabbing his bag, so that he could go say

his goodbyes to the important people in his life who cared about him. He sat back down, though upon remembering that "There are no important people in my life that care about me. I kind of forgot to make that happen, I guess," he went on. "I mean, I've been busy here with the abyss and all and, well, I don't know, just forget it, okay?" So, without any guns blazing and with legs entirely untangled, Wilson didn't so much plunge headlong into the abyss as he kind of slid in quietly, his sword reluctantly and awkwardly in hand, feet shuffling.

"It's hard not to explain what it isn't like in there. The first thing you don't see is nothing, and then you don't float everywhere and nowhere in the same moment," Wilson recalls after returning a week later, kids in tow. "Or maybe you do all of those things backwards or inside out—I don't really know." At an official meeting of the PTA, Wilson explains what happened while he journeyed through the emptiness. "It's strange to think that I was somewhere inside of each one of you and myself and also nowhere at all in the same instant. It's a funny feeling you get when that happens, kind of a buzzing or tickling sensation. Well, anyway, that kind of thing went on for some time, days, weeks, years, I can't say really—and then things took shape. It was still a huge unending nothingness all around forever and everywhere, but if you looked at it a certain way, it was also maybe like a field or plain or some quiet place.

"In fact, it was the *same* darn field where the abyss and

61

my booth sit, but none of that was there really, just the empty field. And your kids, they were there, too, suddenly. And also they weren't at the same time, but the important thing in the end is that whether or not they were also not there, in some way they were there just as much as they weren't. I tried to hold onto that.

"And so, I see these kids, your kids, and I think, great, now all I've got to do is get the hell out of here, but then I don't really know how to do that so much, so it was a dilemma. The strangest thing, though, was just a short stroll across the field, me and these children of yours, we found a big sign that said: *HELP, PLEASE* right on it, and beneath it there was like this little button, and, being in need of help, we went right on ahead and we pushed the button. There was a kind of crack noise, or bang, or whip or something, and then we looked back to where we had started and there we were standing down the field, a-whole-nother set of us. Me, the kids, it was all the same. We were there at the help button and we were also over there down the field. You get a kind of funny feeling when that happens, when you see yourself in front of yourself, and I'll tell you what, we were kind of scared, you see, about the whole thing really, and we figured it had to be a bad idea to meet up with yourself like that so me and the kids just kind of up and got the heck out of there. We started moving across the field, trying to keep our distance, to get away from them. The thing was, though, pretty soon they were following us just as fast as we were leaving them. And off down the way there, we could kind of make out a whole other set of us following *them*. Far as I could tell, they weren't following us so much as they were trying to get away from the third set of us that was following them, which got us to thinking that maybe we were making a chase, that maybe we weren't just running away from ourselves, but that we were also without even knowing it, chasing our selves. The proof was in the pudding on that one, you see, because we thought, hey when we get up to that hill over there we'll stop running, but before we could even do that, well, we saw that we already *had*. That is, up on top of the hill, lighting a little campfire, was *another* set of us, the one's we had unknowingly been chasing. So, we sat down there on top of *our* hill, lit our own little campfire, and then down back behind us, lo and behold, another little campfire lit up atop a hill we had passed earlier, and then it was all pretty clear that stretching forever in front and back of us, there was us huddled up and afraid to go forward or backwards. We were surrounded by ourselves and paralyzed by it. The funniest thing, though, was that a little while later, one kid says, 'Hey, you wanna get out of here?' And we all kind of agreed that, yes, we did want to get out of there, and who knows how, we kind of just did. Zipped right out of there. And that's how I saved your children from the bottomless abyss of nothingness."

"And Ms. Anselar?" a parent asked.

"Yeah, couldn't find her so much." Wilson admitted.

The PTA thanked Wilson for his time, gave him one fruit basket instead of two, "on account of you didn't really do the whole job without bringing back Ms. Anselar, now did you?" and sent him home. The next day, everything went pretty much back to normal. The kids were back in school and Wilson sat in his booth doing next to nothing.

Once, the abyss made a kind of farting noise and a dead cat fell out of it, but other than that, things remained quiet. "It's okay really," Wilson says of the abyss, "I mean, I look back on my life and I think, well that sucked, and I look forward and think, well that's gonna suck, but then I sit here staring into the nothingness making $7.50 an hour and it's all right. Sometimes," he whispers, "it gets scrambled porn. You know, like on TV? You can only see it for like twenty seconds at a time, and you gotta watch it all day to see it, but you know? What else is there? Scrambled porn or nothing, right? Get it?" He laughs.

64

KISS MY ANNULUS

$$A = \int_r^R 2\pi\rho \, d\rho = \pi(R2 - r2).$$
— W.B. Yeats

$\int$

Ringing phones start too many stories.

Take this one for example. When it rings right at the mouth, we are forced to consider others that open this way—those crime novels, that translation, some classic, a romance, the paperback. And we wonder how to react to it happening again, here. Ring, ring. Are we angry? Bored? Do we write it off as cliché, played out, done? Or do we forge ahead, like a cocksure gymnast swinging from one ring to the next, remembering similar openings as generally worthwhile?

Or, hanging on the sound, do we pause to consider why it's such a common technique? Is it the sense of mystery? The call to action? Laziness? High probability? Phones are ringing everywhere, from bedrooms to submarines—why not at the beginning of a story? Is this cynicism?

Or is it, like bells, an affirmation? Of hidden things,

like funerals or weddings or Sundays? Of a place that's only real between the time when the ringing starts and when it's answered? An imaginary place where everything is possible at once, vibrating *phono*, sounds waving in and out and from one thing to another?

But isn't sound, like a spooked herd of gazelle, a thing that spreads outward from a point of conflict, in all directions? Yet this only further illustrates multiplicity, the array of options opening up to us—it could be anyone and anywhere—rushing away from danger, suddenly.

That sounds nice!

But a ring is also singular, an object placed around a finger—a promise, which is an engagement, which is a constriction. The phone keeps ringing, and it grabs us, encircles us, tightens around us with a kind of caged hope, an optimism drafted in the belief that, with so focused a direction, something good has got to happen, finally, so don't let go. Follow the karats, jump through the hoop.

And we answer it, both the story and the phone and everything else, not because we are actually hopeful, but to find out—in the spirit of all too many engagements—whether or not we are wrong. About what? Doesn't matter, we are always wrong—though often in ways we haven't thought of yet, which is a poor reprieve. "Hello?" we say.

At first there is only static, a muffled shuffling, like a pillow smothering a sock. "Hello?" we say again. We bristle excitedly. Anything could happen. And then there's nothing. Not even a click, just nothing. The ring is empty.

The number, too, is unfamiliar.

+

Oh well, you think, forget the call, time to go over finances.

You place your tax returns on the desk (pressboard) and retrieve the bills collected in the kitchen (linoleum tiled). You chew the relationship between the two (dreadful), and then compare this against a list of available funds (liquid and solid). You feel a mix of shame and anger at these digits (0-9) because it is only when dealing with numbers, infinite though they are, that the finite world flops back down, like meat onto a counter. God, remember when the phone was ringing and everything was possible? That was great. *And now these numbers.* There is no way to compete with numeracy, only the means to applaud it, meekly. It is a spectator sport, and wins races and runs companies. Galileo turned Dante into astrology with maths, tossing the rings of hell into orbit; what have you ever done? Narrowly avoided bankruptcy?

Bravo.

It's at this point, as always (if you double-check, you'll see that this is true), that you become uncomfortable being the subject of the story. How did it happen anyway? Wasn't this about all of us before, or at least everyone else? Now it's just you? Get out of here. It's all too specific and a bit trivial, even snide. And barely accurate. Yet, whether it's mundane, dishonest, or even mildly antagonistic, you admit it doesn't seem to be changing. Now, *open the bank statement.*

69

Thank god, the phone is ringing again.

Ooooooh! You answer it too quickly, forgetting to savor the brief precipice of possibility, and fall straight into the familiar canyon of a loved one's voice, asking you if you want Mexican or Thai tonight.

Ugh. The riddle is solved, the mystery over. The lens has focused, the image cleared. Fuck: no more ethereal hope bells. No more possibilities. Only regional differences.

You feel a pang of disappointment. Then guilt. Why opine the absence of an imagined stranger upon the arrival of an actual loved one? Is the unknown more appealing to you? Pig! Just start talking. There's not much to say, but say it anyway.

Now: Mexican or Thai? For some reason, you hedge around these two, trying stupidly to dredge up what little uncertainty lies between Mexico and Thailand. "Um," you say, considering the Pacific, "well..."

Then—yes! You can hardly believe it—you're getting another call, the other line. Fidgeting, you admit to being curious, but not thankful, though to whom you're admitting this you can't be sure. You'll admit it to whoever's on the other line if they'll forgive you for secretly relying on them, or if they'll carry you across a chasm you don't understand and which in fact doesn't exist. Wait, the Pacific? "Hello?" you say, clicking over.

And then, talking to you, almost too quickly to comprehend, is someone offering both forgiveness *and* a ride across unknowable and nonexistent chasms, in as much as thinly veiled real estate scams amount to all that, which they usually do, and for a competitive price to boot.

There are condos at Rates You Would Not Believe.

There are People Just Like You changing their lives As We Speak. Great! What are you waiting for?

You politely ask this person, who you now notice has a kind of sexy musk-laden voice, to add you to the do-not-call list—despite the endless coastlines, European architecture and astounding APR. "And your number is?" they ask, which is strange, considering they called you. But you give it to them anyway, if only to hear it repeated back in damp, dulcet tones.

And then, clicking over, you're answering, "Mexican," while secretly weighing supernatural realty equities against your impotent check book and imagining that sultry voice materializing in your living room as a blooming genital spilling over with peppers and ground beef and desire and boundless wealth. "No, wait, Thai," you say.

And, like a gauntlet, the conversation turns suddenly to *when* and *where*. Christ, the certainties are really adding up now. Time. Space. Distance. Speed. Volume.

Jesus, *surface area*.

"7pm," you barely manage to shoot out. Whew.

Relief doesn't last long, however, because your loved one throws all caution to the wind, saying, "How about eight? I have some errands to run." Errands? Eight? You can barely process this. You just want the phone to be ringing again, to be about to answer it.

Then, like a guardian angel, that blessed beep—another

call, this time somehow answering *you*. Is it the musky service rep calling back to say your voice is sticky too, to drag you through the ear piece? Oh, you can only hope.

Clicking over, however, there's not a trace of musk, only dull rhythmic thumping that increases in decibel and rate. And underneath all of that, something else—a genderless and desperate scream, over and over again, knifelike and real. It too is getting louder and more hopeless, like a dog that learns language but gives it up after judging speech too inadequate to express suffering. There are not enough buried bones to embody it; a whole new realm of terrible possibilities is blooming out there. You don't even say hello, merely click back over to space-time and love.

"Eight sounds good," you say, shaking.

—

And now—poof—a date, 8:30pm. The clatter of plates, silverware. A surprise change of heart: Italian. Wooden boardwalk as marimba. Inaudible chatter. Sea breeze. Clams. Jazz. Laughter. Lights, couples, gulls, and hair blown gently from faces. A tide coming in. The service here is poor, but no one is screaming. The wine is provincial, but no one is in pain. Or at least they're not flaunting it like new scarves or fancy hats.

Which is only polite. What kind of person dials a stranger and dumps their anguish on them out of the blue? It's terribly inconsiderate. There are prescribed numbers for everything. When hungry, call Pizza Hut. When sued, call a lawyer. When troubled, call a department: police, fire, technical support. Do *not* put it on a stranger. And it follows that if someone hasn't called those numbers, then they aren't actually in trouble. It's as if that call didn't even happen. A comforting thought! Yes, *it happened to someone else.*

It's almost too easy, he smiles, grabbing a hand from across the table, thinking of someone else.

Who? Musky Meat Mouth? Maybe. Admittedly, he cannot block out entirely the memory of that call, nor the inhuman howling. His mind circles back to it at inopportune times: dessert, the mention of a sick relative, a compliment. When his date steps out to the bathroom, he checks his phone, stupidly. What was the number of that call? Staring at the screen, he imagines a movie plot wherein he dials that last number only to hear an ominous ring from the purse across the table. How maudlin. Then, in reality, he registers a peculiar fact.

73

All the numbers were the same. Something sticks in his throat.

Three calls. Muffle. Pitch. Scream: each originated in the same place. The weight of this fact barely registers by the time she returns, smiling.

He eats distractedly and talks coolly, but only at first; soon he's drawn into routine. Not forgetting, just floating, as if the evening were a mid-afternoon drive to nowhere, with him in a passenger seat, the third person, while a potentially sinister world simply sails safely by, out the window.

It's while they're fucking later that the phone rings.

And it's *her* phone this time, a thirty-second pop tone looping through the room. Had she purposefully placed it on the bedside chair? He doesn't know, but can just about make out the LED display, glowing over the socks and old magazines. Unfortunately, the number is obscured. He doesn't answer it, of course, but keeps thrusting the two of them along the sheets, closer and closer, inch by inch, trying to get a better look.

658, okay—and, is that a 4? Or a 7?

The numbers blend together as if working to other purposes, as if adding up whatever it is that accumulates each time people sleep together. How much do I have, he thinks, and what is it?

9? 718? The ringing fills the room, jarring and arrhythmic. People, too, are rings, he muses like a fool, but he hasn't the slightest idea how to answer one, so he keeps going, sliding slowly toward a revelation. It looks like it could be the same number, maybe. Just a little closer. But before any kind of arrival or epiphany, the ringing stops, the glow fades, and the room is left darkened and silent, save for the sound of a nameless thing pointlessly accruing.

×

Then factors multiply. That is, things change. For one, I can't fucking take it anymore and go to the police. I'm surprised to find myself at the center of whatever this is, and I don't know how to proceed, or even how I got here, really. The buoyant and attractive officer registers my anxiety with a wry smile, though I can't be sure this is in my favor, or in his, or someone else's altogether.

"So, let me get this straight," the officer says, "You got a call from a number, but it didn't connect." I nod. "And then, you got another call, from what you now know to be the same number." I concur. "And it's some kind of real estate offer?" A scam, I say. One of those pyramid schemes. Like spam. "Isn't spam on the computer? Anyway, then you ask them not to call again, right?" And I give them my phone number, I say, that's important. "Is it? They clearly already have your number." Exactly! "Hmm, and then, you get another call, again from the same number, with a lot of noise and something that could be a scream, like a dog but a person?"

Right, and then it got louder. "Okay, and afterward you went on a date? And your girlfriend got a phone call? And maybe it was the same number?" Yes. "But you don't know for sure?" Before I could check, she caught me going through her things, trying to guess her cell phone password, and broke it off with me. "I'm sorry to hear that, sir." It's okay, but now what? "Oh, well—I'd try a dating site, I guess." No, about the number. And my credit card, like I said, which has been cleared out. "Oh, that. Take it up with your bank. Otherwise, there's not much to go on here. I can call if you want, but that's about it. Neat story, though."

The police are useless, and my cancelled card is tangled up in litigation and red tape. But when the system fails, it's time for good old-fashioned American ingenuity. Grab the bootstraps and fly. For wings, I've invented a story that keeps

75

me going, pulls me along, a fiction wherein the musky sales rep is borne into a secret, shattering Condo bondage, all for merely letting one too many contacts slip into the dark crack of the do-not-call list, and that, through some deranged logic, she thinks of me, of all people, for help—not only because I was the catalyst for her incarceration, no, but also because we shared some undeniable intimacy, rare in this world, unforgettable even in the red-glossed throes of a bloody and sadistic pummeling.

This is my bootstrap.

The story is a bit flimsy, and in fact completely false, but something rings true enough to keep me going, so I do a little research on the internet, dig up some dirt. The numbers lead me from old leases to private holdings, distant bank accounts to poor credit scores, nebulous websites to unregistered phone numbers, from angry forums to storied comments sections, and finally from deeply buried "About" tabs to one Annulus Equity Marketing and Management, a small company located in rural Dry Prong, Louisiana, a town, or village really, founded two hundred years prior, around a water mill whose principal river source dried up each summer, leaving the town financially unbalanced and clawing desperately for stability in an unforgiving and alien landscape, a legacy that may or may not have left its people innately prepared to take on just about any scheme, Ponzi or otherwise.

I hate these people from afar, imaging a kind of hillbilly meth lab that conjures money from trace elements, like modern alchemists, warlock financiers.

I have my reasons, too: the current enterprise stinks more than I previously suspected. There's nothing concrete, but I sniff out ambiguous turd after unspecified plop, all stinky and congealed. Annulus, for example, crops up in more than one missing money case, not to mention numerous allegations of identity theft and fraud. They're tied, if only tangentially, to a ring of misleading business ventures meant, it seems exclusively and almost blatantly, to take advantage of people, their ambitions, and finally and most importantly their money and property. A few of its primary figures are currently serving upwards of twenty five years in federal prison, though stamping them as officially part of anything would be a legal mess not worth attempting because all of these incriminations amount only to patchwork threads sewn together through blind guesswork, vague news reports, old court filings, peripheral public tax indexes and sideline property records. But the tone is there, a disembodied voice screaming over miles of unlabeled telephone wire for *my* help. The bottom line? I've got to get to Dry Prong.

77

Musky meat voice, I will answer your call. I am A Person Just Like Me and I am changing my life As I Speak.

÷

Driving across the Mason-Dixon Line is like diving into America's underwear. It's sweaty and thick with growth, and ever more so deeper into its counties. The south has an impersonal and detached way of being itself, despite the reputation for friendliness. Hospitality may be true of its people, in a greater degree than can be expressed through anecdotes and travel journals, but the landscape itself is different—or, more accurately, *in*different, even arrogant, with its green swaths and endless vines taking over everything in its path, like it owns the place, which perhaps it does.

Dry Prong, the village, is no exception. It is surrounded on all sides by a latter day American jungle, a billowing green mesh of trees and swampland and thickly knotted bushwork, cut through by hairlike waterways, streams, springs and creeks, some sullied by distant industry, lone factories and shipping/receiving centers, while others remain mysteriously pristine. Yet, time worn or resilient, all call out in unison: *sorry, don't care, busy.*

So, when a driver from up north comes snooping into town, as if to save the Princess from certain danger, Dry Prong takes little interest. Dry Prong lets the man walk about peeking in windows and loitering because Dry Prong has better things to do. Like what? Like sitting, resting, aging, warming, cooling, raining, drying, counting, tilling, and growing and dying.

Who else but Dry Prong is going to hold that house in place? Who else will push the wind across the concrete blocks of that abandoned apartment building? Who else is going to admire the useless mill as it nobly gathers dust and families of rodents? And who else will take on the tedious work of sitting quietly in the town center, as if referee to a boxing match between long-closed shops?

No one. The answer is no one.

It is only out of the goodness of its heart that Dry Prong shows the sneaky man an empty model home and an old office. And Dry Prong doesn't mind when the man crawls into the forgotten Condominium Complex, "A Private Community," because what will he find there beside the Annulus Realty sign, graffitied with obscure obscenities? Nothing else but foliage and emptiness. A few muddied toys, sure, but no stories of how they arrived here or why they need privacy. There are no stories in Dry Prong, only blank pages, defiantly filled with grammatical errors and scattered in the street.

But when the stranger oversteps his bounds by breaking and entering, kicking a door in, Dry Prong goes from indifferent to wrathful. First Dry Prong takes out the man's car, with a flat tire, via broken glass, and then Dry Prong sucks the man's wallet dry, at the mechanic and the motel, and then Dry Prong takes his dignity when it attacks and beats him outside of a bar, though it doesn't require much to do so, just a few kicks to the ribs and face, a few broken bones and maybe a concussion, very little effort for a town whose weight trumps that of its inhabitants a million fold, amounting to a lopsided boxing match held in a ring that is Dry Prong itself.

So it all too easily leaves the man adrift, far from home, broke, hospitalized, fee-laden and without a soul to care for him, in a place where the water has run thin along with its population and opportunities, and it doesn't care that the man pleads he's "only trying to help someone in need," nor that the man has made nearly no progress at all in doing so, save

79

for being in the general proximity of the fiction he aspires to. Ha! But Dry Prong, though vengeful, is not wholly uncaring. It prefers an even hand, so Dry Prong kindly offers the man an olive branch, the only way it can—in the form of a job. At Annulus Equity Management. As a telemarketer.

Σ

They assemble.

Together, they march into the second floor office. They wear hair curlers and cargo shorts. They gossip about soap operas and child rearing. They're here for the money. They are here because the bowling alley closed. Because their grandmothers are sick, because their dog has diabetes, because a television program is cancelled, because time is running out, because it's raining, because someone lost a leg, because the opportunity presented itself too many times, because it's fun, because of snacks.

All too often, it's the snacks.

And they are divided into sets. They're rushed toward the forums section, where they are instructed to friend-request at least fifty people per hour, and to consistently upload nearly-nude profile pictures, not of themselves but of anonymous women, women surmised to be Russian or Uzbek or Korean, not specifically but generally, if that is possible, and as if this were some kind of an apology for everything, though in the end, the women are just as apt to be American, and no one is sorry. They operate under the belief that "there are plenty of hornies out there" and everyone wants free

porn. No apologies are made—and to whom these apologies
might even be directed remains a mystery. To their mothers?
Themselves? Who cares, they say, just add me, add me.

Or they are cordoned in the ROMS and emulators
barracks, a makeshift office in what used to be the supply
closet, where they aggregate the digital images of every video
game known to man, crossbreed them with feigned news
reports about the health benefits of acai berries, and make
them available for download in the hopes of driving traffic
through briefly lived sites crowded over with ads about
abdomens and legs, like insects—themselves often created by
other departments. Also, more porn here, indefatigably.

Or they are shuttled to the email department, a huge
hive of activity, where they'll write free-form poetry and
heartfelt letters from fictional Nigerians, to better strut
through the gates of email filters and ultimately net more
personal information, zip codes and social securities and
drivers licenses, as if information were the direct product
of probability, which perhaps it is, or they will sit in rooms
where videos are uploaded, graphs rendered, Powerpoints
structured, codes written, and they will contact other agents
in an expanding ring of entrepreneurs, among whom they
will, at higher levels, herd finances and financers toward
shaky land markets, both in the states and abroad, through
gentle nudges and tough prodding, promising booms and
busts, braying as if the transcontinental railroad were about to
be rebuilt across once useless towns and counties and sections
of the internet, each now destined for an unprecedented future

prominence in a World Beyond Belief Where Not Everyone Can Win But Why Not You?

They try to find the melting point of every object and hyperlink, like monetary alchemists squeezing rocks and html until gold and paper pop out. They do so without meaningful regard for profit, casually allowing others to use their methods, letting money funnel gradually off into anonymous accounts, perhaps out of carelessness or stupidity or apathy or, though unlikely, a rare camaraderie and sense of empathy. In large measure, too, they are often calling on themselves, swindling different portions of their enterprise one day, another the next. They not only offer Inventors Tool Kits, As Seen On TV, but they buy them too, wholesale. They acquire their debt. They redouble their interest. They catch their tails. They are unaware, however, that they have been infiltrated. They do not notice themselves, at least in very small part, traipsing through the hallways, looking. They do not feel themselves spying around corners and through doors left ajar. They remain unaware that the smallest contingent of them, namely one, persists only out of an inexhaustible determination to rescue a fictional woman that, despite (or due to?) being only a figure of their meek imagination, remains frustratingly elusive. They do not know that they are still trying to win, because, well...*win what?*

It's only when we pick up the phone to make our first unsolicited call that we realize we've come full circle.

82

^2

We've been gone for a while and need to take stock. We hear the ring we've made, but no one answers. We can't help but feel the same way we did after our first call—empty, hollow.

Why? We spit Ouroboros' tail from our mouth.

Despite all the voices we've heard, *she* is still missing.

She isn't in any of the utility closets. She isn't in the unused gymnasium or the boiler room. And then, when we find her, we admit: well, not really, no, we haven't, because she isn't real. We have not unlocked a conspiracy any larger than a few idiots skimming bucks off the top. We have not untangled a dangerous web of illicit activity in which women are shepherded into dire sexual misadventures. We give up.

But then, unforeseen, she is sitting next to us. Great!

She is huge and sudden. She rolls out from her own body like flour from a ripped bag. Really, she doesn't sound at all like the woman with the musky voice, or the screamer. In fact, she is neither of these women, nor even the one we imagined them to be. She is someone else entirely. But as with so many before her, we let her stand in for what we want. A placeholder occupying a pronoun and a body. She works here, too, has for much longer than us. She has gotten used to it— in the same way that we begin to think she's what we've been looking for anyway, that we were wrong before, that she is it. She takes us home. When she has sex, she splays out across the bed like a half-melted chocolate. She smells of uncooked chicken, neither appealing nor offensive, but overwhelming and occupying. Afterward she discusses what she knows about Annulus as if reciting bad poetry or deciphering a poorly crafted horoscope. She's been in almost every Annulus department, and she imagines that things are more organized than they at first appear. She views Annulus not as cynical but as an absurd affirmation of something that remains unseen. She says that they are not con artists but patriots, not thieves but heroes. She is delusional. She says that it's all like an equation, the economy and our lives. She smokes inordinate amounts of cigarettes. She keeps saying the word equation as if to multiply it, or divide it, and she says there must be balance. She does not mean this in terms of moderation and restraint, but literally with regard to equal sides, as in the case of scales, as in how much gold is equivalent to six hundred thousand dollar stores, as in how can we tip the weight against trillionfold stimuli, as in a train leaves Dallas going sixty miles an hour and to what degree does this obfuscate our dreams? She says we keep growing and moving outward, that we have to, it's natural, but that, since it is an equation, something has to be added to the other side to keep everything from being flushed out through the equal sign, like so much shit and paper and hair, though she does not clarify where any of the sides are located, nor where things might be flushed to or how. She says that in math the equal sign is an anus. She says this again and again. She is excited by it and usually wants to have sex again after she thinks about it. She says we have to turn everything into money and credit as a kind of colonic

84

blockage system, to render a lasting stillness in America. She says spam and scams are a kind of financial-peristalsis liturgy to be spoken by a chosen few. She watches too much television and has as much to say about American Idol. She does not understand my incredulity. She gets angry when I make my own metaphors. She says it is not a metaphor. She says there is an enormous hole through which real value can actually be lost. I ask her to show it to me.

She does.

=

First off, it can talk.

Have a bloody mary, it says, gesturing with a twitch of its muscles toward a makeshift bar. It's in the water mill, where it somberly gurgles. It is round and pink and fleshy. It is a hole, yes, but it is crowded, and it brings to mind uncooked hotdogs and raw sausage, bisected like oversized pepperoni. But it's not dry. Rather, it appears buoyed as if by a brine, floating in the center of the room, like a meaty donut hung by strings from the rotting rafters, and it is wet and leaking. Every now and then, the dark hole at its center is revealed by the parting of its veiny membranes.

You can sense it defiantly smiling.

You want to talk about what she told you, about the equations, about scale, but don't know where to begin. You want at least to ask about the musky-voiced woman and where she went, or if she's even gone.

It talks instead about bacteria and how cute they are.

85

It talks about the ones living in the Mississippi River, that they average 8,000 microbes per cubic centimeter. It says that it would like to see a new Huckleberry Finn, starring effluent water and *Vallisneria americana*, common hydrophytes. Gut flora especially are its favorites, and it imagines Twain's new narrative exploring rivers within Huck's pubescent body, his esophagus, stomach, large and small intestines, colon. Bacteria are too often maligned, it says, with antibacterial soaps and antibiotic pills, yet the entire body would collapse without them, the forgotten organ.

Eventually, it asks us how we feel about the story ending this way. After starting with a mundane ring, it wants to know, is there balance in a non-existent and floating math hole? Or does the narrative need more grounding, more reduction?

We aren't sure how we feel yet, but reduction is good. Give it more time. But what, it asks, could be more reduced than math?

No, we disagree, math is 100% abstraction.

That's not fair, it says.

To be honest, shouldn't we be talking about people, not numbers? About home owners, not functions? About retirees, not equations? About shareholders, not dividends? Or, at least, about sex, not sums?

People aren't constants, it says, they're variables.

That's a little hard to digest, we say, and you're a real jerk. Stop doing math.

It begins to pucker itself in retort, but moves instead

as if angered, then hurt. It begins fluttering, shaking what might best be described as its lips. *Fine!* it manages to mumble obnoxiously just as it's overcome with a heaving thunder. From underneath the thumping and gyration spills a familiar scream, real and hopeless. And then, as if to affirm the fact that speech is an inadequate release, there's *the smell*.

Oh, it says meekly, Pardon me. And you do—with a kiss.

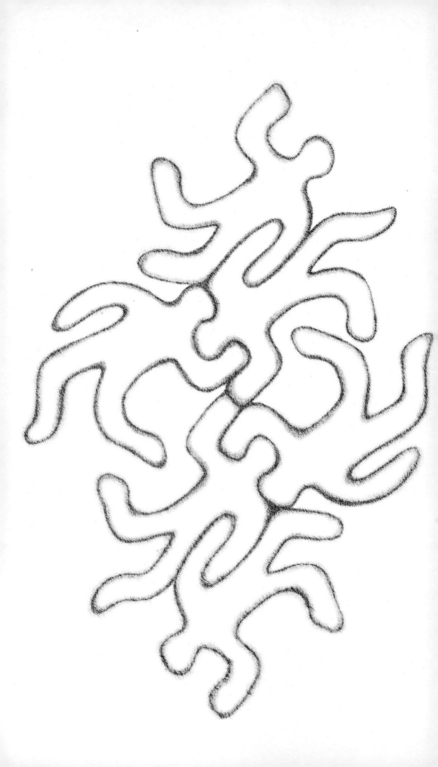

THERE ARE PLACES IN NEW YORK CITY THAT DO NOT EXIST

There are places in New York City that do not exist. Fresh examples are found every day. There's no conceivable limit to what they may or may not contain, and now these unreal rooms, vaults, buildings, shafts and tunnels are the subject of an investigation being undertaken by Pratt Institute. The impetus for the project remains, comically, a hundred-year-old Brooklyn ghost story.

As is so often the case, it begins with a curious newspaper account, a sarcastic 1894 *Times* article about Bushwick (a "rocky, bleak, lonesome district"[2]), wherein the area's most notorious ghost is depicted as "a woman, who goes about in the scantiest of attire, with disheveled hair and bare feet, and falls into a fit of hysterics as soon as any one approaches."[2]

Though five petrified women swore they'd seen her and a "calcium light" in November of that year, most likely the ghost was just a cold and raving drunk, one more casualty of the booming alcohol industry that so defined the neighborhood in its youth. Skepticism aside, over two hundred men still set out to kill, capture, or exile the apparition in the middle of the late autumn night. Yet nothing appeared before the angry citizens beyond their own breath and chatter. After shuffling back to their beds and daily routines, the woman was all but forgotten—until a rogue investigator returned her to the spotlight.

"He declared that while walking across the lots near Irving and Knickerbocker Avenues," pursuing an exclusive interview with the drunk/ghost, "he was confronted by the spectre, who performed the serpentine dance while he remained rooted to the ground,"[2] immobilized and unable to complete or even begin his line of questioning. Imagine a plastered hobo subduing a reporter with her languid, swollen rumba—what impossible moves could make a man confuse a woman for a ghost? Whether reinvigorated by this attack on Freedom of the Press or excited about the prospects of a New Dance Craze, a mob of over three hundred strong— including a police task force and patrol wagon, numerous citizens armed with "rusty old army swords," and even one man "arrayed in fragments of an ancient suit of armor" (of which "the breastplate did not fit him very well")—stationed themselves together as a mighty Bushwick battalion to finally run the spectral woman out of town, swiveling hips and all.[2] It's a classic NY scene: so many strangers gathered together in costumes and accessories, hoping to catch a quick glance of their own deaths before them, a theatrical end dolled up in spectacle and circumstance. They failed, of course, but not

90

for a lack of trying. That is, if "trying" in NY means milling about empty streets into the wee hours, talking into a corner and waiting for your life to change, which it does.

Rather, city officials themselves claimed credit for her expulsion, saying that "there is not to-day, or, rather, to-night, a place in the city of Brooklyn where a ghost can walk without being run in" because "a general order was issued, directing the Captains to be vigilant and rid the city of apparitions, spectres, and all sorts of ghosts."[2] Though obviously tongue-in-cheek, the accomplishment is no less astounding or profound; that ghosts are not real serves only to make more amazing the police department's success in eradicating them. That is, it ought to be impossible to do anything at all to nonexistent entities, such as ghosts, yet the officers still managed to usher them, i.e. nothing, out the city gates with authority. Have you ever tried to remove a nagging emptiness from your life? The task is more arduous than its imperceptible weight would imply.

At the time, Brooklyn was its own urban entity, separate from NYC proper, and the regulations noted above were listed as "one of the reasons why we don't want to have our city consolidated with New-York. If such a dire disaster should befall Brooklyn, all our anti-ghost orders would be rescinded, and our streets would become haunted night and day."[2] That Brooklyn has since been incorporated as a borough of NYC is firmly established and incontrovertible—and that the non-existent ghosts therefore have returned in order to not-haunt the streets is merely a matter of deductive logic. Zoning and county limits have changed in the dead's favor.

But where, exactly, are (or aren't) they?

To put it bluntly, the dead have been priced out. This is easy to imagine, considering the rising real estate prices in Brooklyn, "with the average price per square foot rising from $421 in last year's third quarter to $443 this time around,"[4] and that the average income of a dead person is abysmally low, remaining unchanged for centuries at somewhere around $0 annually, not to mention the unemployment rates in this demographic, which run at roughly 100%, depending on the year. Nor is this a weak attempt at humor or levity, but instead a sad and unchangeable fact.

If America has an equivalent of what the Indian caste system calls "the untouchables," it is the dead. We are not allowed to interact with them, to employ them, to wash or bathe or feed them, to date or even kiss them, and we are told to regard their very existence as suspect. Becoming dead all but eradicates contractual agreements and nullifies marriages. They have almost no rights and can't even vote in a country that calls itself free. A few among them are revered and given preferential status, but these dead-to-riches tales of stone monuments and enormous murals are anomalies that serve only to veil the inequities so endemic to the population.

Like many outcasts with nowhere else to turn, the dead may very well have taken to the streets, homeless and destitute. Yet, reports of hauntings in the city are at an all time low, and those made in shelters and hostels are often revealed to be the grumblings of the mentally unstable or the scared whimpering of traumatized children. Much of this remains beside the point, however, given that ghosts and the dead are hardly allowed lodging at all in shelters or even hospitals—as soon as they're discovered in these places, they are sent off to be buried and hidden from public view. Yet, this is a clue: looking for them underground is a place to start. Traditionally, the most reviled and exiled of New York's pariahs take to the network of subterranean spaces that stick like mollusks to the bottom of city infrastructure. With nowhere else to turn, the ghosts may have taken residence in the abandoned subway stations and platforms, the bricked over rail lines, boxed in developments, roped off storehouses or barricaded drop shafts.

93

The most comprehensive popular report on such places is Jennifer Toth's *The Mole People*, a book that describes in detail much of the lived in, searched over, and rumored infrastructure beneath the city. Though widely read, much of its claims are, according to scholars at Columbia University, patently untrue and blatantly falsified. This embellishment is disappointing, especially in the search for lost ghosts. Oh, how desperately we want to believe in "the secluded tunnels that run beneath the busy streets in an interconnected lattice of subway and railroad train tunnels, often unused now, that in some areas reach seven levels below the street,"[5] all running outward, waiting to be discovered and explored, a whole city mirroring our own, both empty and full of hope, but as we plow through the earth and our dreams every morning, we must face the fact that "there are rather few unused sections of tunnel, and they are short," and we must consider how much "work and expense it takes to construct a tunnel," and how much "documentation in the form of corporate charters, franchises, contracts, bond and stock offerings, and news reports of construction" there are, letting all of our romantic notions deflate and collapse under "studies, public hearings, annual reports, contract bids, and other public record."[1] No, the vast warren of limitless space does not exist, neither underneath us nor even anywhere. The places simply are not there. This is what makes non-existent spaces the most valuable real estate in NYC. Their not being there doesn't mean we cannot look for them, cannot hope to find them, or wish to be in them, finally, but only ensures their lucrative supply/demand ratio. In an amazing feat, the supply is so low (zero), that it can hardly achieve the demand (infinite), a demand borne out of our longing to believe in something just out of reach, something waiting for us around corners and over hills, a spectre hoping to dance us into stillness, impossible people and places stretching outward from the paths we pad over repeatedly, something to shake off the feeling that this is it, these stairs and platforms and doors and vesitubules, archways, atriums, and halls are the limits of the world, the end of the earth, such that nothing could ever be more expensive than these dream places, their unimaginable prices bordering on myth, or fetish or religion or the place where all of these things meet our ambitions in a dance we don't understand, a tango, a buck-and-wing or cabriole, a "vigorous rhythmic dance originating with Gypsies," a "sinuous Polynesian dance with rhythmic hip movements," a "Breton dance resembling a quick minuet," a quadrille, rigadoon or samba, a "dance where partners move around each other"[3]—all of it, everywhere, mocking us not with its deadly living, but with its never occurring, never happening, never existing and simply not being, not here or anywhere, the one thing we can never really have, to not be, so meet me on the corner of Knickerbocker and Irving, because—if only out of spite alone—we too should assemble to kill it, again and again, right where it isn't, until it lives.

Bibliography

1. Brennan, Joseph. "Fantasy in The Mole People." Abandoned Stations. Columbia University. Web. 20 Oct. 2011.

2. "Brooklyn Ghost? Phsaw!." *New York Times* 23 Nov. 1894. Web. 20 Oct. 2011.

3. Chrisomalis, Stephen. "Word List: Styles of Dance." The Phrontistery: Obscure Words and Vocabulary Resources. Web. 22 Oct. 2011.

4. Polsky, Sara. "Real Estate Industry Issues Quarterly Notice of Rising Prices—Market Reports—Curbed NY." Curbed NY: The New York City neighborhoods and real estate blog. Web. 22 Oct. 2011.

5. Toth, Jennifer. *The Mole People: Life in the Tunnels Beneath New York City.* Chicago: Chicago Review Press, 1993. Print.

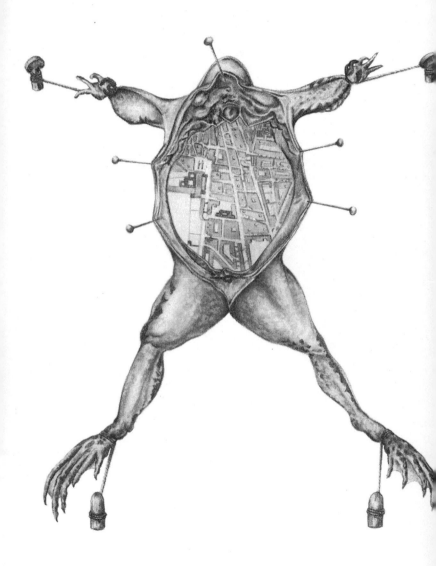

ANATOMY OF THE MONSTER

Our ship arrived at dusk. Spanish moss cast warm shadows along the moorings. Straight away, we met with government officials, quaint reactionaries usually found festering in Town Hall. As the doctor's assistant, I took notes while the mayor detailed all we'd missed.

"Here, rumors are common, rarely trusted," he said, nibbling at his cheek. "And so initially, the monster hadn't seemed so threatening. But then came stories of its swift approach, inhuman abilities, moral apathy: towns leveled, organs eaten, children raped, bodies heaped, societies erased, et cetera, et cetera."

The doctor and I shared a glance: this wouldn't be the routine leeches/tinctures affair we'd expected.

Before the monster's actual arrival, the mayor remembered, townspeople dripped with anticipation. None could certify its existence, but all wondered how the government planned to safeguard against the idea of it. The mayor said he was "loath to spend funds on fibs pedaled by vagabonds, ne'er-do-wells, and tramps." Only after a drumming in the polls did he pivot away from a platform of practicality, sighing with the knowledge that legislating from absurdity would be even easier than the usual constraints.

"Selectmen," the mayor said, "deliberated to no end." By scrutinizing the town's layout and commissioning expert advice, they proposed defenses ranging from catapults to militias to packs of wild dogs. But rumors and gossip always undermined their delicately calculated security. *"A moat?* The monster loves swimming. *Fire?* In some parts, it is fire. *Arrows?* They adorn its skin the same way a hunter wears a bear-tooth necklace—tauntingly." The monster, in its ambiguity, adapted to every attempt to fortify the town. But, after a night of heavy drinking, in a rare moment of clarity, the mayor proposed that to battle an abstraction, they didn't need specificity at all—no, they needed gross generalization.

By this stage, my notes were becoming increasingly complicated.

"We needed something all-encompassing," he said. "A blankness upon which all permutations of the monster could hold." After months of adjusting knobs, detachments, turrets, and oils to fit the exact idea of the monster, the selectmen settled on the simplest and most uninspiring of defenses: a wall.

We saw it as we approached the harbor, surrounding the town in a long gray arc. It had taken over a year to build.

"Imagine us atop its steep embankment," the mayor

said, and affected a far-off stare. "*We were all there on the day of reckoning.* An entire town standing, wondering if all we toiled for could buffer the unparalleled force finally bursting from the forest"—he jumped from his brown leather chair to animate his story—"in undulating waves stretching nearly a mile across, obscure, vein-hooded body parts sloshed toward us the way racehorses alternately overtake one another out of starting gates—stutters of flesh converging in mixtures of unbroken velocity and sudden crests." He wiggled from one foot to another, swinging about the office, hair and jowls swaying like flags. The doctor looked on, stern and unencumbered, while I struggled to record not only the mayor's words but also his movements.

99

The mayor grabbed a lamp to further demonstrate the scene, waving and shaking it. "Parts falling forward like tentacles thrown down in loud slaps upon calm water. It snaking from trees, renting branches and overwhelming shrubbery in storms of dirt, mud, and leaves. Louder and louder, its calls ascending toward crescendos that never come." The mayor let out a series of shrieks not unlike a cawing crow, and the doctor nodded along in polite understanding. "One scream after another raising the ante again and again, like an unhinged and riotous cattle auction that's less about livestock than some underlying anger, bidders staring each other down amid rising stakes and uncertain intent."

"I stood frozen," the mayor said, locking himself into place, "in a special type of terror. We had prepared for anything, but the monster wasn't just anything anymore, and, in the face of its being so precisely itself and nothing else, how could our wall—a mere generalization—still hold it at bay?"

The mayor struggled to catch his breath, exhausted, and melted into the patterned office wallpaper. As he blathered on, I looked down at my notes, distracted—inky scribbles and odd shapes crowded the pages like stains on a fat baby's bib. Obviously, their wall had worked but solely because of a peculiar fact: *there was no monster*, only a bunch of people working some kind of mobile clearance sale, nomadic mini-mall, or roving corporate flea market. In fact, we had seen it—or them, really—at the foot of the wall, while touring the grounds en route to the mayor: "How are you today?" they'd exclaimed with too much expression. "Do you need any help with anything?" they'd yelped with a glee betraying profound sadness. They were all hawking something: contracts, memos, and brochures flitted around like bees. I was more than a little confused when someone first pointed to that group of people and called it the monster. I almost blurted, "Where?" but instead kept jotting in my notebook about the charming masonry and archwork that gilded the quaint homes and buildings, loose shapes sketched among names and quotations. While our investigative team snatched some much needed rest, the doctor and I went over the notes, piecing together the mayor's story by lamplight. Taking a bite from his large slice of cake, the doctor picked up where we'd left off: "The mayor, peering over the edge of the wall, still not grasping what was actually down there, probably declared, *We did it! We stopped the beast!* and the delusional townspeople no doubt erupted in screams again—this time not out of fear, but joy." He took an enormous bite of cake and continued through his chews, "After the initial euphoria of survival wore off, however, they lost direction. They hadn't anticipated the space beyond victory or defeat. Nervous, they wondered: *What now?*"

In subsequent interviews, the baker explained that the silence and uncertainty broke when the fishmonger shook, "We have to kill it!" Others agreed. Instantly, a team assembled itself to usher the monster into oblivion. Armed with a rifle, three swords, one hammer and a large rock, heroes climbed down the wall into the vicinity of the newly calm beast. It looked as if the thing might go out peacefully, but then in a flurry of movement, sensing the presence of the townfolk, it reared back into full motion, writhing and flapping about. Brave and daring, with a surge of energy and with images of their families and friends in mind, the group of men descended upon the monster in a glorious attack, shooting knobby mounds of unnamed flesh studded with blenders and accessories; eviscerating a teatlike appendage adorned in brightly colored travel magazines; and crushing the bulbous node atop a flank, somehow smiling at them and waving to unknown purpose.

Of course, our inspection of the crime scene told a different story, revealing the mangled remains of one paid spokesperson, one Tupperware salesman, and one acne-scarred clerk, each still holding various clearance items. The villagers had no idea. Even more unsettling, it appeared as

101

if blood and bone fragments did not deter the "beast"—no, so far as our forensics could tell, the people constituting the monster had come jostling forward in knots and mobs through the carnage, intent on selling this or that to the would-be warriors. Trembling at the memory, the baker explained, they had just barely managed to clamber back up the wall and pull their flimsy rope back over the ledge before being overtaken by its enormous claws or—as the Doctor suggested, needling his shrimp plate—*clause.* "Right," the baker nodded, confused.

Conventional methods could not kill the beast. That it must therefore be killed by unconventional means was obvious to everyone, the welder told us, but what methods of killing an unimaginable (*only* imaginable?) monster were conventional? Chopping off its head? Bleeding out major arteries? Gouging eyes, removing skin? Any of these might have passed an unconventional executions test for humans, but for a fantastical beast? Who knew? And besides, who could even say what part was foot or skin or artery? And if they couldn't pinpoint body parts, how could they sever them in unseemly ways? A decision: they must understand the anatomy of the monster before establishing coherent plans of attack, conventional or otherwise. They'd almost lost good family men in their first attempt and could not risk repeating the same mistake.

That's when, via smoke signals, the doctor was called. His job? To label the beast.

Now, with the doctor standing triumphantly along

the ramparts, the mayor thanked and deferred to the much-needed authority. By reputation he knew the doctor's methods were exact: products of elite and mysterious training. Remorse lingered under the mayor's smile, though, because the doctor, as is customary, bills his time by the half hour—and he is *always* on the clock. And though the doctor moved with an intensity that looked casual, he took as much care with each observation as he did when inspecting grand meals. He rarely touched a piece of meat without invoking a series of equations and figures. I wondered how he planned to broach the subject of the village's delusion or confusion, but in the flurry of events, I didn't ask. The doctor had a way of assuring that he knows what he is doing, and that you know it too, even though what he actually does is unfathomable and unknowable.

103

He didn't shy from producing results though. Leaning over the parapet with two fingers of whiskey in one hand and a cup of garlic spinach in the other, he proclaimed, "On this day, let it be known that the veil has been lifted, the monster unsheathed, if only partially."

And with a gesture rife with pomp and ceremony, he announced the liver.

Beneath him, the liver squirmed around with their hands in the air, each figure enacting some promotional dance or jig.

The doctor displayed no intention of disabusing anyone's misconceptions about the monster, and in fact gave these misconceptions names and identities, each drawn from a nomenclature based on solid but complicated reasoning.

Here among the unseen barbecue grill hawkers was a lung, over here with the unknown frozen meat deliverers was the suspensory ligament of the duodenum, and over there among the overlooked pharmaceuticals and beauty aides were scattered some subclavian veins. On and on, the doctor paraded himself, waving his hand like a wand, magically proclaiming so many people and their jobs to be organs and ancillary parts. I asked the doctor whether or not we actually planned to help these people—because they seemed to be suffering from widespread delusion—and, to me, it felt like maybe we were feeding into it? He smiled and asked if I had failed to tell him all these years that I was, in fact, also a doctor. Then he continued on his way without hearing the answer, of which there wasn't one. That night I found a plate of beef Wellington on my pillow, accompanied by a note that read, "Rest easy. We are helping. That we might also make a little money along the way? It cannot hurt."

104

The mayor ordered the townspeople to return to business as usual: "Yes, an enormous monster may be just beyond the stones of that wall, and yes, it appears to be lusting for blood, and yes, we know nothing about it and are only barely being rational in believing that the wall can hold the thing indefinitely, and yes, it does dwarf the lives we lead with its omnipresent reminder of death, but please return to your daily routines as if nothing has changed because, if you think about it, besides all that, nothing has." And so, shops reopened, bakeries fired up ovens, people started making purchases.

By the time the doctor's procedures had hit full stride, however, the entire town was in the throes of something like a communal midlife crisis. The doctor denied noticing it, but through a secret network of mirrors and echo-capturing funnels installed by our court of investigative assistants, I observed the slack jaw of the woodcutter pausing over half broken logs, apathetic soap swirls painted upon the barkeep's mugs, the wilting frame of the postmaster, slowly slumping into the soil. In interviews, villagers begrudged themselves: *There's more to it than all this.* Their revelations were trite, but the townspeople, in a wave of self reflection, were equally aware of this stupidity and cried that recognizing the futility of malaise was not the first step toward something greater— but instead the last lock barring them from it. Though each villager's misery was different, one chorusing question was common to everyone: *What did the monster think of them?* They swore us to secrecy, looking from side to side and sweating, unaware that everyone else in town shared the same secret: all were making private contact with the beast.

105

I tracked their trysts through reflections and echoes. Small irrigation and sewage ducts speckled the wall's base in regular intervals, and one by one, the people began slipping into these tunnels for a closer look at the monster, seeing whatever it was they thought they saw. Watching the beast, the townsfolk resembled giddy children rolling in summer grass. In fact, it was a teenage boy, Eric, who first heard a voice, who first communicated with what *should* have been an as-of-yet-undiscovered organ of an enormous non-existent monster.

"Hi," it said to him in the voice of a young woman. "Have you given any thought to a life insurance policy? And are you protected in the event of a fire or flood in your home?"

Through a corridor of over a hundred and thirty mirrors, I just barely saw the boy jump and stammer, "Wha— who is that? Where are you?" Mortified, flailing at walls and steel bars and grates, trying to ward off anyone who might discover his inviolable rendezvous, he scrambled out of the water tunnel back to bed, breathing heavy, full of shame. He'd been caught doing the unthinkable, unaware that almost everyone in town also had a special time when no one would notice their absence. Just as much, he was unaware that it was the beast itself that had spoken to him, though of course, again, the beast did not even exist, so it wasn't that at all. He was wrong about knowing *and* not knowing it. I made a point of following his movements—repeatedly, he'd sneak away, hear the voice of a woman offering "fiscal and monetary shields in event of unforeseen disasters" and run, terrified, back home, too ashamed to notice everyone else's crippling shame. He spent days narrowing eyes at everyone he encountered, measuring the possibility that they might be the person who had discovered his secret. Yet, he never heard that distinct voice in town, a voice that he admitted was beautiful and alluring. Even I felt so, and I'd only heard it ricocheted along hundreds of walls. Eric couldn't get it out of his head. Eventually, he gathered the courage to stick around and respond honestly.

"I have no idea what you are talking about," he said into

the darkness, "but I like it. Who are you? Where are you?"

"I'm talking about a simple investment in your peace of mind," she said, suddenly timid too. "And I'm right here." Eric couldn't see from inside the dark tunnel, but the boy kept talking, determined not to run home, drawn in by the comforting cadence of her words.

"What are you doing out here?" he asked, half afraid she might ask the same of him.

Her voice continued to lose luster, but replied, "Just hoping to help you feel comfortable knowing your assets are well protected—so you sleep easy." The boy was enamored, as if he'd always wanted someone to feel this way about him—to care for his well-being, to want him to sleep easy—though he might have imagined it a bit differently before now.

107

"I feel the same about you," he said, in a way that sounded not so much like he really meant it but maybe more like he believed he eventually could. Their conversation continued through the night in much the same vein, a mutually misunderstood but comforting volley. They were still at it when the sun began to rise. In the pink and orange light of dawn, she said to him, "You deserve comfort and security and I can give you that," but Eric started to really wonder—*where is she?* In all this new light, certainly he should be able to see her now. Yet, to him, there was only the beast.

And when he finally discovered that she was actually, according to the doctor, a set of toes, he was at first furious and later even a little disgusted—he abhorred feet—but in the end he accepted and even embraced it, the power of their connection overwhelming his prejudices. He told her, boldly, that he loved her. The sudden shift in emotions, the hairpin turn that the relationship had taken, caused a snap in the toe, or perhaps a final stitch, visible, to me at least, as a quiet tic in her left eye. She'd been broken or fixed and started right in: "I have no idea what I'm saying or doing. Really, it just kind of comes out. I don't think I'm a toe but maybe I am. I don't know how I got here. I don't even know my name or what insurance is, or if it's one word or three, but only that I have to sell it to someone, somewhere—anyone, anywhere. What does insurance even look like? I couldn't tell you, but I have to make someone buy it. Why? I don't know, but I don't want to find out what will happen to me if I stop trying. There's something bigger going on in here, I can feel it. People whisper to each other. Rumors spread. We don't know what's true. I can't trust anyone. I don't remember if I had family or even who I was before I woke up here, chasing a deadline. I'm scared out of my mind. There's some kind of force, a feeling in here, a combination of people and ideas. You can catch glimpses of it out of the corner of your eye when people gather together in huddles—talking, planning, thinking. That's just it, too—it's got no physical form, it's an idea that I can't even grasp, it's too big, the type of idea that only ideas themselves could understand, and not individually but collectively, a group of ideas coming together and thinking about an idea, and the idea they are thinking of is looking for something that only an idea's idea could desire. What could an idea want? If it's insurance, then I could help, but beyond that? It's not my job to think about this. Still, I do and I'm scared. But, Eric, somehow, really, you make me feel safer, though I can't imagine why. You make me feel like there's something beyond this idea, beyond the paper and beyond the insurance, but what? The way you talk, it's like you're standing and looking at me from a point of view I never could have imagined. Like you're standing outside the world and peeking in. You seem to understand me even less than I do—but the more you don't know about me, the closer I feel to you and the nicer I feel because the farther I can get from where and who I think I am, the better. I don't care if I'm a toe. I'm your toe. Or, at least, I'd like to be. So just, please, for the love of everything we know to be true, sign these goddamn papers and set me free." In a rush of intimacy and misunderstood affection, Eric signed all the documents and ran excitedly through the pipes with papers spilling into walls, white sheets falling like dander or spores. I had to laugh when he called out into the night, "I am insured!"

109

I immediately briefed the doctor, but he insisted that Eric's was an isolated incident. It was not isolated, however—budding relationships between the beast's body parts and the townspeople were reaching secret pinnacles all over town, deals made with unknown currencies. The doctor conceded to me this point but then chided my verbosity and countered that isolation was a broader concept than I realized. "The voices of the beast are not only not toes," the doctor told me, "and not only not lungs and not feet and not necks," (I was having trouble getting all this into my notes) "but they are also not penises and not vaginae, advertising and business being a complex but complete sexual act unto itself, as you know, like a slit starfish...and as such, being separated even from itself, it's quite isolated."

I found these remarks curious, to say the least, but the doctor assured me they were mostly in jest, and even that he'd ponder my concerns further, as a favor. I was surprised then that the doctor, upon completing his detailed labeling of the creature, held a meeting in the town square to announce that, according to *my* notes and graphs and maps, the beast could not be completely understood—at least, not within the limits he'd previously been working, because, "Apparently, and perhaps unfortunately, the town itself appears to be contained in the beast's body. That is, the town is part of it, or actually a series of many parts, and—I'm only giving you facts as they become clear to me here—beyond medical explanation, it appears to be pregnant. With itself." That this was an absurd and utterly incorrect reading of my notes hardly mattered at all. "Obviously, we dispensed with the truth a long time ago," the doctor said to me while dubbing the town water mill a tonsil, the first designation in a new campaign of labeling and naming different parts of the village itself, citizens included.

Understandably, tensions rose. Previously, the monster was (somehow) visible to the townspeople, but now the doctor labeled things they hadn't expected to be monster at all— and so everything became suspect. Tables? Chairs? Cabinets? Gardens? Anything at all could be—and probably was—a part of it. No one wanted to be the horrible beast they all feared, and who knew when the doctor would knock on *your* door and file you away as an artery or knuckle? Perhaps he'd say your home was a useless gland? Or, God forbid, a patch of unseemly hair? Obviously, there was a type of pride in being a pivotal portion of the central nervous system or large muscle, and the town clerk, a major artery, did more than a little gloating in front of the innkeeper, an extraneous gonad, after the doctor swept through their neighborhood in a flurry of names.

Eric saw these developments as an opportunity— sneaking the toe through the wall and into town was no problem now that everyone was just another monster part. To demonstrate devotion (to each other? to the idea of insurance?) they made a habit of going door to door, hand in hand, selling something they didn't understand to people they didn't know—just because it felt nice.

Though Eric and the toe enjoyed a boom in sales, an underlying competition was slowly being nurtured. People resented each other and their labels. Plus, they were all already delusional, so it all kind of dawned on me at once that things were getting starkly out of hand. How had it gone this far? The doctor was roving about the town in his robes, followed by a retinue of cooks and attendants and women. He was like an overstuffed Gestapo, instilling fear and trust at random, sowing uncertainty and ill will like robust crops. Having exhausted, down to the smallest trinket, new things to name, the doctor ignored rising pressures and moved on to where the womb might be located. He suggested, "Most

111

likely, it lurks underground somewhere. I've seen blueprints of the tunnels beneath the streets—we must investigate down there. This may help us derive limits of the monster's body—and our own, as the case may be. Besides, I suspect our limits and our womb are one and the same, seeing as we are pregnant with ourselves."

We? Our? The doctor was suddenly including himself in all this nonsense? I was taken aback, but he assured me, "Given the circumstances, I think people find it comforting that I am a nipple, one more part just like them. And you," he said, "you are a nostril, one of ten." I tried to remind him that, in fact, I wasn't, but he insisted, regardless of whether I was or wasn't, in some way—I was. "Think about it," he said, before handing a crude map to the mayor, who then contracted a team of townspeople to dig beneath buildings.

Three groups left from different parts of town, moving in different directions according to the doctor's calculations. One group later emerged, muddied and sopping wet, from the harbor; another trekked in from the foot of a mountain, citing lack of proper tools to continue; and the third never returned, lost in the tunnels they had dug that burrowed on and on into the darkness. Each claimed that they couldn't find any wombs or limits, but that they'd seen "other things." Like what? They wouldn't say.

Unsettled, I again tried conveying my concerns to the doctor, but my notes were jumbled and I always stumble with improvisation. Mostly, I just pointed to doodles and loose phrases scattered about pages piled in my chamber, a room

112

that had become increasingly harder to navigate, while the doctor looked at me like I didn't understand how much money we were making. I understood more than he realized, and the fact that the townspeople were getting poorer and poorer did nothing to assuage my fears that something terrible might happen. The mayor and most government officials had been labeled warts and other blemishes, some only temporary calluses and blisters, and everything had been turned on its head (now a local, nearsighted school master). Alliances formed among various body parts. More powerful organs and lesser subsystems armed themselves against one another. Fingernails and wrinkles banded together with ear lobes and calcium deposits in attempt to make demands of the spinal cord and hippocampus; the brain hemispheres, along with major systems, plotted out means to keep lesser neighbors under foot (a downtrodden cobbler). Small skirmishes erupted in the night.

113

To boot, the baker (or adrenal gland) and a woman (hangnail) selling lifetime supplies of stainless steel kitchenware, had consummated their love by entwining business ventures. In an alliance meeting in the northern pub, the baker proposed, as a method to overcome opposition, a series of wild business ventures that would "redirect the flow" of something left unstated, a sort of commercial union or ménage à trois/factory-farm to package and distribute a feeling, a kind of tangible emotion they could hold that would manifest as some vague change in the town and their lives. It was very clear to him, which was well and good, except that the people he loved had become not only the products he sold, but the people he bought them from and also his body parts and the landscape around him, all amidst what was slowly becoming a full on war in the town.

In a final plea to the doctor, I did my best to outline the havoc we inflicted on these people, but he just looked at me with genuine eyes and half a smile slung low across his face, whispering, "Oh, you really are the heart of this operation, aren't you? Up in that chamber of yours?" He sighed, "Maybe someday you *will* be a doctor," then patted me on the shoulder and looked me in the eye. "Don't worry. The cure is working. In fact, believe it or not, the townspeople are in remission! It's a miracle. I plan to make a report of it all tomorrow."

Then the doctor killed the monster.

I watched it all from my mirror chamber. Instead of a formal progress report, he stormed into an alliance meeting the following day and announced as he entered that he'd found the womb. "It's love," he said. The crowd turned in silence, giving him full attention. "The womb! It's love!" The doctor, for perhaps the first time, was nervous, "And, and, the uh, child...*is us!* Like I said. But more than that, too. It's friendship, and family. I mean, baker, look at you! You're happy! You have purpose. And Eric, the boy? And his beautiful toe friend? Aren't they an inspiration? A lot of good has come of this, really."

Something was wrong. This wasn't the announcement I'd expected at all. Running through my notebooks, I ran fingers along trails of numbers, added dividends and tabs.

He continued. "You thought it was going to eat you! Or kill or rape you! Isn't that a laugh? Hindsight, right? Oh," and he forced a shallow snort of glee, fake and nerve-ridden, "to think it would have turned out as nicely as it did. A new camaraderie is forming, I can feel it."

I blended data from town records and far-strung ledgers.

"The womb is producing great offspring among us, truly," he said. "I see a bountiful future, a new beginning. And if the womb is a myth, which it is, does that matter? Aren't myths, in so many ways, truth? Didn't you say something to that effect, Reverend, uh, what was your name again?"

"Excuse me?" the reverend asked. "I thought I was the unibrow now."

The numbers came together: the town was bankrupt. It was over.

The baker stood up, squinting: "What are you trying to say here, doctor?" The crowd leaned forward in unison.

Regaining composure—as if all along it had been the holding back and anticipation that galled him, not the coming clean—the doctor smiled, snapped his fingers, pointed at the baker and said with a wink, "Heh, there is no monster." After a pause, he bolted out the door, yelling, "Light the fires!" Through mirrors, I caught flashes of him cutting across town while his retinue poured barrels of oil and pitch from rooftops, igniting streets in huge pillars of flame.

Smoke clogged alleyways and rushed over houses. Mirrors cracked in the heat and the roar of burning wood flew up through funnels, amplified to constant surges of static. In scattered reflections, I saw the mayor screaming for water, for dirt, for help, and people running around like they'd just opened their eyes for the first time, at once angry and fearful. I caught just a flash of the doctor hopping down into the ground, no doubt heading off to sprint beneath the scorching streets through the womb tunnels. He scrambled up through a hole and emerged at the harbor, where I was waiting. He looked at me and shrugged, "Fine. Let's go." Spanish moss and shadows blowing after us, the doctor grabbed a satchelful of sailing accoutrement, descended back into the tunnels, deeper and deeper around innumerable corners, finally reaching a grand underground current. We boarded a small sailing vessel, already stocked to the jib with gold, silver and premeditation, and set ourselves off into the flow. "What about the rest of our crew?" I asked.

"Screw 'em," the doctor said, staring up to the rocks, the other side of which people were too busy drawing pails of water to come chasing. Only the doctor's former employees, who had no stock in the land we left behind, would be standing on banks waving fists in anger. Neither of us mentioned the symmetry of our arrival and departure, bookended in smoke. "Those people had a disease," the doctor said. "We had a responsibility to stop its spread." There was a new somberness in his voice.

We popped into the sunshine after a while, and then rode fast with the wind and current for over a week. The doctor spent much of the journey at the prow, gazing ahead, never looking back, scanning waters and nearby shorelines—

what for, I couldn't tell. He sought something, definitely, and when he found it, made it very clear. "I found it," he said, pulling our boat into a cave. Within, we anchored near a dry patch of rock to set up camp. The doctor needed no tent or blanket, merely unloaded all his riches and practically sat atop, falling asleep in a great sigh of relief and release, as if dropping down dead, his life completed.

We spent some peaceful, carefree time in the cave—the doctor had brought along playing cards—but soon, surviving villagers sought justice. The ocean didn't deter them. No doubt they searched every sea cranny, harbor and bay between the village and our encampment. Warriors arrived, usually one at a time, sword in hand, suited in armor, looking for the doctor's head, ready to claim honor and victory. They sometimes came with sample cases or clipboards or contracts, or catalogs and brochures, but they never arrived without swords and anger. The doctor and I were both frail due to scant fishing in the cave, so we couldn't easily fight off noble knights or gladiators or door to door salesmen, but the doctor had this fantastic cannon, all steel and gears and black iron, and, "because of the risk of infection," he would just blow these warriors away in a huge ball of fire. In the darkness of the cave, it was really something. True fireworks, splattering shadows across the rock face. As soon as the warriors came through the narrow mouth of the rock, arms raised and declaring this or that, they were the easiest of targets. There'd be nothing left but blackened flesh and singed metal and the doctor's ecstatic hooting.

I'd often swim out into the shallows to see if I could locate cannon balls for reuse. I'd linger, wading and treading water, enjoying the breeze. The water was warm, calm. Once, distracted by the wind and the sun and my toes in the velvet sand, I didn't see, from the safety of the waves, a sales rep approaching the cave, whistling and swinging his battle axe, and so I never made the customary bird-call warning. The sound of a commotion and scuffle echoing off the wet rocks roused me and heralded the loud clap of the cannon—and then silence.

Not a single hoot, ecstatic or otherwise.

I returned to the cave carrying a cooled cannon ball, and found first the many burned pages of a collectible catalog, the mutilated body of the salesman, and finally the doctor himself. He asked, mumbling, whether or not I wanted a sandwich, despite having no means to make one, then shifted atop his gold, wiggling his hand around and drooling. Blood started pooling in large black puddles. An arrow rested squarely in his neck. He looked like a soggy, brown banana.

I went outside and jumped back in the water.

Floating with the tide, I looked at the cave, smoke ominously rising from its maw, the doctor coiled dead atop his treasure, bones burned beneath our feet, smoldering ruins of a broken town at our backs. Fire, gold, terror, caves—the scaly-skinned arrogance, the slithering use of education, fork-tongued rhetoric, lumbering greed—a dragon? How could I have missed it?

He was the thing that had slunk into town to destroy

it, not those sales reps. And for what? In any event, it's dead, I thought, but after a minute the whole dragon conceit felt a little stupid, and I just grabbed a gold sack and got the hell out of there. Was there honor and glory in this? Maybe a little, but not much. I sailed to a distant city, then another and another, every one the same. Open waters felt just as cavernous as womb tunnels, all options laid out in front of me like transparent knots of corners and bends. Eventually I simply stopped where I was, some small town here or there, sold the boat, traded in gold for currency, and started a small business selling used musical instruments. I made decent money. Enough to eat out a few nights a week, to lounge with books in the park, or catch some entertainment on weekends with friends. I even started a little family, and could afford to enroll my son at a respectable private school. We owned some land in the country. Recently, too, I ran into Eric, the young boy, and the insurance-selling toe, outside a small market. They were older, obviously, and married. They looked happy. I was nervous at first, but we smiled at each other somehow. She was pregnant. Their clothes were cheap but cared for. There was only a little wind in the air, but it felt right. My hand lingered too long on her round belly, so much so that Eric had to touch my elbow to get my attention. I tried to look into her eyes, and then his, but I had no idea what anyone was feeling. We stood there smiling at each other outside the market like that for a very long time. I didn't want to leave. The market stretched out around us like the sea. How long could we keep smiling? There is no monster, of course, I

119

thought, but I want to be a part of it.

It started to snow. "Do either of you play music?" I asked.

TUNING FORKS

It started as a humming. Charles didn't hear it that morning though, because he was late and couldn't be bothered. Also, he at first hadn't turned off all twenty-seven alarm clocks in his house. Charles didn't like to be late, not at all, because, "it's not something that suits my personality," but he nonetheless made a habit of it. Not that he didn't do his best not to be late—by setting alarms throughout his bedroom and living room and bathroom and car, or by drinking a lot of water and not going to the bathroom before bed—but however punctual he might manage to be throughout the course of waking hours, he still couldn't control what he termed "morning-me" any more than he could control his neighbors or his mother or taxes or the sun. "Morning-me," he told Sarah on numerous occasions, "is not me at all. I'm a completely different person. You know that, you have to know that. Don't you know that? I mean, who is this guy, I wonder, really. Think about it, Sarah, I don't want to be late, right? Why would I? I could lose my job, you don't think I'm aware of this, Sarah? Jesus, I'm this close to losing it, really. But as much as I'd like to say morning-me is the one who faces embarrassment in front of his peers? Well, no, he's really not: it's me. Because by the time I get to work, late, I'm not even him anymore, but me, regular me, instead. Morning-me slips out quietly when I'm not looking, while I'm finding my slippers or cursing something close by. I don't know where he hides the rest of the day, Sarah, I really don't." But wherever morning-me "slipped off to" that particular morning, Charles was not late for work because of him or because of a missed alarm clock. No, he was late—and therefore too preoccupied to hear the humming—because he'd just the night before slept with another woman.

124

He had a small but vivid hickey on his throat and was unsure what to do about it. Sarah had been out of town, a rare occasion, and would be coming back that afternoon. Charles opted to take his razor and cut clear across the purple bruise, hoping it might look like a rough shaving accident. He spent the early morning cleaning up their place and erasing what had happened both from the house and his mind. He'd never cheated before and maintained that he actually still hadn't, that another part of him—a part he detested, really, and would hurt if he could get his hands on—had done the sleeping and the sex and all that, leaving the real him, the innocent him, to clean up the mess. And Charles loved Sarah, he harbored no doubts about that, just as much as he felt that "people who love each other don't sleep around on each other."

If he loved her, then he couldn't have slept with that woman, Alicia, he knew. Someone else must have. It's logic, simple. But in the end that meant someone who didn't love Sarah lived inside his body—which Charles did not like at all. He felt that only he should live there, that he alone crowded up the place enough as it is. On his way to work, in a car stuck in traffic, when he finally had pause enough to notice the hum, by then a kind of gentle thumping, he thought only of "The Tell-Tale Heart"—was this his guilt taking physical form? Or, worse, someone *else's* guilt?

At work, the humming became a kind of buzzing and a whistle and a low grating all mixed up into a continuous pulse, unmistakably coming from outside of him, though he could still feel it in his chest. But Charles looked around the office, and everyone, for the most part, was doing their regular thing. No big deal. It was annoying, the volume of the sound, but that's about it. It was normal in that part of the city for planes to fly pretty low overhead, the enormous sound of their turbines interrupting meetings or bringing chatter to a sudden halt, so even when the noise became more of a steady razor shaped rumble all around?—it was easy to pass it off to the background, just more white noise among the regular cacophony of the city. These things happen, Charles thought and took out the folder for his current assignment.

He'd been commissioned to increase efficiency and morale through ergonomic and atmospheric redesign of company floor plans and office layouts. He originally felt

125

like a glorified interior designer, but his research had been surprisingly compelling. Red wall paint increased accuracy in computation, blue bolstered creativity. Somewhere, he expected, was the perfect shade of purple to meet company needs. His managers had given him quotas, abstract ideas that could be fudged if need be, but he kept in his head an idealistic goal of finding all the right design nuances to maximize productivity. A desk here, a light there, a rug across this section and a series of paintings and bulletin boards throughout—there must be a way to make everyone do the right thing at the right time without feeling any different. In the coffee lounge around 10, Charles asked David, a nice data manager with too much debt and too many children, "Hey, do you hear that? I mean, what is that?" just as easily as he might have tossed out, "Well, how was your weekend?" David's reply, "I know, right? Always an adventure in public service," was an answer to hundreds of questions asked thousands of times before. He barely even looked up from his celery. Throughout the morning, they would suddenly notice it for a moment here and there, but then the sound would slip back down into the undergrowth of the day, a kind of weed in the office that only reinforced Charles's belief that his work in company atmosphere had merit.

"Hey, get this," David said around noon, actually having to yell a bit. "I'm talking to a friend of mine online here—she works downtown—they've got the sound, too. It's all over the news." Charles didn't know what to make of that—a few times, there had been mystery smells that wafted through the city, thousands inexplicably sniffing maple syrup or Kool-Aid, or both at the same time, but he had no reference for an omnipresent sound. David returned to his celery, of which he apparently had a never ending supply. Charles imagined David standing outside of himself, a body double handing him stalk after stalk. An hour or so later, Meredith approached them and passed a note onto Charles's desk. He read it and showed it to David: "I think they are going to evacuate the building." It was only a few seconds later, though, that Liana, the new proofreader, soiled herself. She just lost it while making copies. A line of brown liquid slid out of her skirt and down her leg and she kind of buckled over. David and Charles both stood up, but she ran from the room toward the bathroom. In the hallway, a few people they didn't recognize were running to the bathrooms as well, holding their bellies. One guy, an intern or temp, vomited in the water fountain.

David said something to Charles, but he couldn't hear him. When had it gotten so loud? Charles knew it was louder than earlier, but he couldn't place when it had happened. Through the noise, they heard a screeching, a shrill line cutting its way up to their ears, struggling to be heard. Across the hall, in the conference area, a woman looked down at herself, having dropped a ream of paper, shit running down her legs, and she screamed, her mouth open wide, but it barely amounted to a whisper inside the suddenly huge sound. The sprinklers came on and the exit lights started flashing. Everyone reacted simultaneously in a flurry of jackets and phones and bumping elbows. Almost instantly, the whole company was moving down the concrete stairwell en masse as EMTs ran up against the flow.

Outside, the sound remained unchanged. It wasn't louder or quieter as they all stepped into the streets and sunlight, but exactly the same. A few people held their hands over their ears. Others were standing face to face, screaming at one another to be heard. The other buildings on the block were emptying as well, a constant stream of people flowing onto 3rd Ave. A fire truck pulled up, most of the men heading straight inside Charles's building, but there were other trucks for other buildings. One fireman stood on a crate and readied a megaphone. He spoke into it, but no one could hear him. He dropped back down into the crowd of people and reappeared minutes later, now holding a large white board and a marker. He scrawled out the words *GO HOME* and waved it around, gesturing stiffly with his hands. No one reacted right away, as if the sign was meant for everyone else except themselves, or perhaps because they didn't really know how to react to the authority of black marker on poster board. It took a minute to settle in, but eventually they realized they needed to listen to these hastily printed words.

David managed to convey that he needed a ride, and when he and Charles reached the car, the head and taillights were flashing. In fact, so were the lights on most cars. Alarms had been tripped by the vibration, but they couldn't hear any of them in the sound. Throughout the city, there must have been thousands of alarms that no one took notice of—what once would have made people jump to action now lost in a

128

sea of hisses and bleeps and drones. By the time Charles and David got going, the traffic had clogged up on every street and they were moving about ten feet a minute—but if people were honking, they couldn't tell. Charles honked for the sport of it. David appeared to laugh, then turned on the radio, the volume way up. He pretended to browse and pick a good station, but what he landed on might as well have been static or silence. The sirens of ambulances and fire trucks were completely useless. They came so often and so quickly that everyone pretty much kept to the side of the road, a third lane created in the middle of the street.

The sound had an increasingly metallic quality, Charles felt. As they finally started up the on-ramp of the Queensboro Bridge, Charles picked out hints of twanging cables, taught saw blades or steel whips. The wait was long, monotonous—thousands were leaving Manhattan over this bridge—and Charles began to sort of tune in to the sound. There certainly wasn't anything else to listen to. As it started to silently rain, he noticed nuances in it. There were no discernible patterns other than its endlessness, but within there were nooks and crannies of pitches, waves and breaks of rhythm. Charles remembered hearing from someone or reading somewhere that perception can warp white noise into almost any sound, a running shower to be confused for a cell phone or loud music mistaken for the doorbell, but nothing in particular stuck out to him now. As the car slowly plugged along over the bridge, drops silently pounding the windshield, the radio blaring unheard, all he could find were random screeches and the unending rumble.

In Queens, police were directing traffic, which struck Charles and David as strange. It's not as if the street lights were obstructed by the noise, but there was a lot of confusion. Charles wondered how the cops were communicating with each other. Those walkie-talkies were just hunks of metal now. He imagined officers standing at their posts, never knowing when to move to the next place, waving cars along into eternity. When Charles dropped David off, David waved and jokingly made a "call me" gesture. They laughed, but it was also a moment of uncertainty or finality or both. It took another hour to get home, normally a ten minute drive, and when Charles got there, Sarah wasn't in yet. She had texted him earlier letting him know she was on her way from the bridge, though she no doubt had been slowed by the thick traffic. Who knows how long it would take. On the armchair by the window, he found a long black hair. Alicia. He scoured the house and found three more, then looked at his puffy red neck and felt stupid. The cut stood out like a forgotten prune—he'd made it more obvious, he knew it. Sarah would know immediately. Charles sent Sarah another message asking how far she had gotten. Still on the Brooklyn Bridge, she said. There's time, he thought and settled into the house as best he could. Plates and papers had been jostled to the floor by the subtle vibrations of the sound. Everything was slowly moving, he realized, millimeter by millimeter, ready to come off the table or counter. It all looked normal in the house, just shaking lightly and quickly, too fast to see. For a moment, it made him a little dizzy. Charles sat down on the couch and instinctively turned on the TV. The news on every channel covered the sound from every angle. The anchors just sat there not moving, the words they would normally have been speaking displayed in marquee beneath them. At first Charles didn't understand why they had the anchors there at all if they weren't going to speak, but when he imagined the news stated in Helvetica on a black screen, it made him nervous and uncomfortable. Seeing the people there gave some sense of things holding together, shaken but still on the table.

They explained, or wrote out, the concept of the "brown note"—a frequency at which some people become incontinent—and they explained, or someone did as the news anchors looked on blankly, that this noise was happening all over the country and some parts of Canada and Mexico. It appeared to have arrived with the dawn, quieter now in California but getting louder. "Experts" made guesses about its origin, but most were just floundering around, tossing facts in to see if they'd swim, and nothing held any water. The waves were too big. No one mentioned the rest of the world, and terrorism was an option but an unlikely one given the scale. In contrast to what the news portrayed as a major catastrophe, the president didn't issue a state of emergency, but instead made a statement that nothing merited alarm—technicians were handling things smoothly across the nation. People were flustered but largely fine. Charles was surprised that things were holding together so well, but then again it

131

was only noise. While he waited, his mind drifted back to the sound again, almost as if it were a separate place he had tentatively approached but still hadn't built up the courage to completely enter yet—he would step through the door, peek around tentatively, then head back out to more familiar things like couches, TV, and self loathing. He ventured a little further into the sound, felt his way around in the darkness of its pitches and harmonies. Really exploring the sound required a type of blindness—or at least a complete re-centering of the senses—and trying to discover what was hidden in it felt like walking with hands on the wall, eyes closed. In many ways, Charles felt he was swimming through it, not knowing where to go next in its cavernous timbres, but just as much it also swam through him, he felt, a droning diesel engine stuttering out bass notes through his gut, exploring and trying equally to find what's next, something fleshy, visceral, or vulnerable. If it were a race between him and the sound toward a soft center, the sound would definitely win, Charles felt. For one, it had definitely gotten louder, which Charles read as increased power to invade him, to understand or pass judgment on him. And he felt confident that he had more to hide than the sound. Besides the fact that it was enormous and seemingly unmappable in his mind, the sound stood naked in front of the entire country, projecting itself completely and proudly into the ears of everyone, while Charles, on the other hand, had a pile of secrets under his skin that he hadn't bared to anyone but the mirrors in the bathroom, and even to them only rarely and a piece at a time. Yet Charles believed there was a version of himself that was exactly who he believed he was, somewhere.

He texted Alicia, the woman from the night before, and looking around the room, saw that a few books and plates had crashed to the floor, unheard. Or rather, of course he had heard them, but Charles was hearing so much that he hadn't noticed. He was sweeping up the glass when he felt a hand on his back. He whipped around, jumping, to find Sarah almost crying. Charles only briefly thought of Alicia, at first expecting to see a pair of forgotten underwear in Sarah's hand or even a series of condemning pictures taken by a hired PI. But her hands were empty and trembling. He let Sarah rest her face on his chest, his chin on her head. Sarah's hair was thin and light and smelled the way Charles often thought of her, clean, comfortable and sweet. He resolved, like a thousand times that day, to kill the him that had cheated on her, to not let him answer Alicia's text if she sent one back. The sound mocked his decision by staying the same, just louder and more profoundly the same, just as Charles suspected he couldn't change, no matter what he wanted to say he'd do or not do. You can't control other people, he thought. Charles smelled Sarah's hair and ran his fingers over her cheek and felt a sense of comfort because right now, at least, he was exactly who he wanted to be, if he just closed his mind to everything else, no matter what came before or after. In this moment, Charles felt, the sound was wrong.

Things were normal that night. He'd done a good job cleaning up his other his's mess. Sarah showered, Charles made dinner. She kissed the cut on his neck to make it better. They passed notes to talk, and read next to each other on the couch. They watched a movie with subtitles. He fell asleep watching her drift off. They both woke up in the middle of the night, the sound now much louder, but they fell back to sleep in each other's arms, Charles still watching her chest rise and fall. He felt better when she was there, he realized and tried to hold onto the feeling. In the morning, the news reports were strangely vague. They seemed to be talking in abstractions. *The sound is taking its time*, they said, or *Some children have gotten lost in the sound and parents have formed a search party*, or *While riding on the sound, a car crashed on Highway 1*. Charles wasn't sure he knew what any of that meant or if the anchors did either. Yet, it was news and it was still there, which the president, in another statement, reminded all was a good thing, not to be forgotten. He told the country, always in subtitles as he looked assuringly at the camera, gesturing with his hands, to take some time to recuperate, but to return to work the next day, to not let this impede the progress of the nation. *WE ARE STRONGER THAN THIS SOUND*, he said. It occurred to Charles that, despite his good intentions, that sentiment literally was not true. The energy needed to sustain this sound spoke to enormous power, much more strength than anything he could imagine. Sarah suggested that, if it were to last, they could generate electricity from the sound. Charles wondered if the sound would let them.

Over the course of the next few days, the sound got slowly and steadily louder, though never as quickly as on

134

the first day. The news suggested ear plugs and told of a sort of sound-related irritability syndrome. The distracting and annoying sound enveloping everyone was apparently too much for some, and its effects varied from complete angry breakdowns to mere snappy comments or overly callous gestures. People were inexplicably not themselves, they reported. Sound irritability syndrome, or SIS, was in full effect. Charles spent only one day back at work, but there, people were constantly lashing out and apologizing afterward or screwing up their work and having to fix it later. Suddenly, everything was excusable. The things people did were not their own actions, they felt, but a mix of them and the sound together, and since everyone already accepted the malice of the sound, it made sense that people were behaving badly. The context of their situation was at the root of the bad choices. As he attempted to push forward with redesigning the office, Charles wondered if, before the sound, it had been just the same—that is, was there an atmosphere, a tone, separate from the one people were used to, that would have been more conducive to better choices, that would have made everyone a better person without even trying? Maybe there was a sound, he wondered, that would make us do everything right, every time. And of course, maybe there were sounds for everything—ones that could make us love or hate or garden or embroider or play shuffleboard.

135

Charles stopped going in to work because a building in midtown had collapsed, falling into two others, luckily killing only hundreds instead of thousands due to heavy absenteeism.

The sound was suspected as the cause, and structural integrity became questionable everywhere, especially in large buildings standing tall like enormous tuning forks in the sky. There was a mass exodus out of Manhattan, but it happened slowly and, of course, quietly. The news anchors stopped coming in, and the updates became increasingly vague: *The sound watches us listen to it, reports scientist*, and *Millions of dollars floating in the sound wait to be constructed*, and then later things like, *Water is available for consumption in cubes and angles*, or *Listening to ourselves, the animals reacting, camouflage*, and finally, *The sound is somewhere here or there but quietly louder*. The president stopped making appearances. After a week, the news stopped altogether as well. At first, commercials kept playing in an hour-long cycle, but eventually that stopped too, leaving only static to match the noise. Alicia sent Charles a message saying, in a long and rambling text, that she may have forgotten a hairbrush at his house. He searched for it, but found only that it was too hard to concentrate.

The sound gave everything the air of an old photograph, of stillness and quiet. Out the window of Charles's apartment, the street was just a still shot of a neighborhood, the homes and hedges overexposed like sudden cuts in a cheap film. Everything stared back, the buildings and roads and lights and hydrants and trash, through a roaring fire no one could see. Even when a car drove by, which was rare, all movement appeared in flashes or juts or stutters, as if the sound had flooded the world in a thick, invisible sludge. By that time, too, it had gotten so loud as to defy logic. They were hearing things in it, distinct things, messages and memories and music and lies. Its ups and downs transformed into any number of things they didn't want to hear and everything they did. At first, it scared them to think they'd never hear anything again, but really, they could hear—they had the sound and they were hearing more than ever before. Charles even felt that it had some therapeutic properties, that it helped him to enter a sort of meditation or even mediation, wherein he might face off with his other selves, meet them and excise them with the sound's blades. He threw out his phone, and Alicia and others along with it, and Sarah tossed the television from the roof and they held hands. From there, they could see fires and looting. Charles heard gunshots, but they couldn't have been real gunshots, he realized, just ideas floating through the vapor. Sarah was getting pretty good at reading lips, or at least she thought she was. She could have been wrong, but it felt like talking. They spent their afternoons tanning themselves in the pounding volume, their skin rippling under the weight of the waves as if beneath a powerful hand dryer. An old man would run through the streets with a shovel, swatting at all of the birds that had fallen to the streets or digging through the trash that blanketed the sidewalks.

137

Sarah stopped washing after a while, they both did, because the pipes weren't pumping. This happened on the same day the sound became so loud that they needed to close their eyes to exist. It took just about all they had to maintain focus, such that the complexity of seeing things was too much to bear, as if the intensity of hearing had now overtaken the limits of one sense and invaded the province of another. They had to navigate the abstract corridors of the sound to keep themselves grounded in something resembling reality, and they couldn't envision the sound's pathways correctly while looking at actual things, so they kept their eyes clamped shut. And they each on their own began a secret relationship with the sound, sexual mostly. It had started while Sarah and Charles slept together, but when it happened, they imagined themselves like separate hands twirling about the clock face of its curves and undulations. Charles felt disgusting cheating on Sarah while he was right there inside of her, but he was undoubtedly more in the sound than in her, and the noise was certainly deeper within her than he ever could be. Neither of them had a chance against that kind of intimacy. How could they get closer to each other than the things that were already inside them? Their sex life went on like that for some time. They crawled around the house with eyes closed, finding food here and there, cereal and bread, and would reach out to each other in the darkness, using one another's bodies as conduits for the sound to rumble through themselves, to get closer to the noise through each other. When the sound briefly and suddenly stopped—dropping away, gone without any warning while they fucked each other to be in the sound—there in the vacuous and hammering silence were Charles's forgotten and ignored alarm clocks, all of them blaring loudly and arhythmically, each one fighting the other for attention. Charles wondered which one of him was about to wake up.

When his eyes opened for the first time in days or

weeks, he found he wasn't fucking Sarah at all, but just a pile of coats by the wall. He looked around the room through bleached light and saw Sarah holding all the blankets on the bed, blindly rubbing her cheeks against the sheets, moaning. What had we ever been to each other, he wondered. And then the sound came back and they kept fucking themselves.

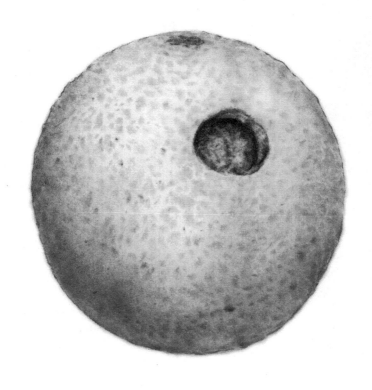

HOW TO HAVE SEX ON OTHER PLANETS

ABSTRACT

NASA is out. Today, privatization greases space for regular entry. And tomorrow? The launch-pad will peddle its cheap shuttles on every street corner. The open void will be erected as a new Bourbon Street or Coney Island, the universe's next rundown, red-light playground. Imagine the greasy, weightless freedom. Lines for The Outer Space, however long and curvy, will be no more trying than those for Starbucks bathrooms on hot, wet afternoons.

Yes, as has been promised to us by movies and books so many times in the past, space will be our coffee break in the future, whether we like it or not—and as with anything else, we will try to have sex in it, whether we like it or not. In fact, we'll do more than try—we will have sex in it, whether we like it or not. If the tourist industry doesn't get there first, porn will—or such is the classic myth in business. Squirters magically fountain over in low gravity, and cocks stretch beyond capacity on enormous masses—the potential is unyielding and so is the profit. The rest will follow.

Heavenly bodies of our solar system will be popular erotic honeymoon spots and debauched pleasure palaces, but—like Hawaii or Ibiza today—each will offer its own obstacles and ecstasies. In ignorance, the uninitiated may at best miss an intimate sensual opportunity, and at worst, crush, vaporize, or asphyxiate themselves. Sex on other planets is, without a doubt, extremely dangerous.

Until such time as there might be more hands-on research, this text, through the guidance of the most advanced astrological and astronomical information, is to act as a speculative guide to the burgeoning and deadly activity of sex on other planets. Have fun, yes, but remember that this how-to is as cautionary as it is leisurely. In fact, going forward, it may be best to think of the omnipresent threat of death as a kind of bonus double penetration, a movement both through you and into the next life, because, probably, you're going to die. Liking it is a choice. So, start fucking. In space.

1. The Inner Planets

We start with the Inner Planets not because they are the closest physically, but because they are the closest morally. They may be called the Terrestrial or Telluric (meaning earth) planets, but they are also the Personal Planets, and as

142

such represent the best initiation for beginners. They care. They are aware of our needs and are "concerned with our feelings...they present us with the opportunity to say, *Yes*, *No*, and *Maybe*."[1] Well, thank you, Inner Planets. While it is still our choice, let's get started.

At 350°F, Mercury is going to be hot, but don't be nervous. This is the land of Gemini the wise! And Hermes, messenger of the Gods! So your induction into ecstasy will be in strong, able hands—hands that can be seen from orbit in the shape of an enormous crater whose troughs spread out like the legs of a spider. Get in there and strip naked, but don't touch anyone yet. Take it one step at a time. Ease into it. There's lube if necessary, but it probably won't be—on this planet, you must fuck with your mouth and your voice. Why? Because Mercury commands all forms of verbal, written and printed communication. Time for mercurial phone sex. Start talking, and fast. Mercury's orbit around the sun is a mere 89 earth days, yet its own axial rotation happens but thrice for every two solar orbits. So you must speak quickly; you and your lover will be years older in a week's time. Say everything you've always wanted to say. Say everything you never wanted to say. Lick your lips and say: "We cannot stop the junkmail from coming, but we do not have to read it."[1] Let your lover say: "We cannot stop the radio announcer from talking, but we do not have to listen to him."[1] If you do this, you will survive the heat, and you will survive the lack of atmosphere and oxygen, and you will survive the intense solar rays, but as you climax, you will come to know that the crater in which you rapidly mouth your desires is named not after Castor and Pollux but after Apollodorus of Damascus, the ancient builder of the Pantheon, and like him, you will be accused of imaginary crimes, convicted and put to death, both by the press and the authorities. There's no fighting the spin here, and unlike Apollodorus, you will not be remembered, as a crater or anything except a stain or a pulp novel. The junk mail continues. And the empty feeling? That's your pantheon.

Now, onto Venus, where it's all pressure and no caldera. A swarming white testis, the tantric Venus exists in a perpetual state of longing and desire, punctuated by sudden eruptions against itself and others. Lacking plate tectonics, for example, the planet holds positions for eons until geology finally bursts outward in hot, massive resurfacing. At ground level, atmospheric density is the highest in the solar system, ninety-two times that of Earth's. Conversely, the naked human body typically pushes outward with a force of fourteen pounds per square inch—a meager effort here. Venus wants to get inside of you—and be warned that Venus shares etymological roots with *venenum*, poison. To successfully have sex here, without entering into a kind of toxic shock, you must blend in, you must be a chameleon—though not of color but motion—and you must commit to a dance that mimics the planet's pervasive lust and repression. You and your lover will slowly subduct across the surface, shaping your bodies into angular forms, redolent of geometric figures and the rocks around you. Be a ballet of stone, mineral, and strata. That is, while gutting striations through the sulfuric desert with palms and feet and knees, one of you must play the role of subductive slab, reaching your throbbing lithosphere into the other's primed accretionary prism, running back-arc basins in taut lines against the other's spreading axis. In order to avoid notice, all of this must be done as slowly as possible. Dancing, you should be as unseen tangents to each other's slight curves, never touching except in ways that don't matter. To onlookers, you must appear naked and completely still, like strangely wrought statues, your limbs cut at unnatural angles into stone, left here long ago, forgotten by your builder, slowly worn away and shorn of color. If one of these onlookers announces, "I invite you in the name of Mylatta," let them take you, both intimately and as a souvenir. Do not move. Do not speak. Do not anything. Hold it in. You will be venerated and revered, displayed and studied. In enormous buildings, academics will pore over you through glass, ogling your paused body as if at an unhinged, post-historic bukkake session. When you can no longer stand it, and at the exact right moment—in tandem with all of your marbled lovers—release, suddenly and with anger. Step down from the pedestal, hips swinging like back-alley switchblades, and be as overwhelming, insatiable, and destructive as you like. At this depth of longing, the difference between mortal violence and orgasm should be, at least scholastically, indiscernible. You are the caldera. After all of this time, Aphrodite—*un grand mort*.

145

On Mars, in the name of war, you will don the colorful masks and vibrant costumes of Mexican *luchadores*. As pro wrestlers, you will tag-team yourselves, flying off the blue ropes into the red, iron-oxide hematite. Prepare for engagement. You will act out the moves of battle, but only as rehearsed. You will tear at each other's bodies and clothes, but only as theater. You will beat and pelt one another, drenched in sweat and passion, but only for dramatic effect. You will not wish "for the actual suffering," but instead "only enjoy the perfection of an iconography."[2] That is, there's no action, only acting. And why do we act? To remember, to look back and codify. There is no war on Mars: all true violence is enacted toward the future as a kind of fevered hope, but on Mars everything is expressed toward the past, a hallmark of nostalgia. If there is a struggle, it is against that of the oncoming future. Violence is motion, sadness an inscription, and here it's all stillness: four billion years ago, the planetary dynamo stalled, halting the magnetic field. The pieces and parts are here but none move, just flaccid bedrock. The central fluids are desiccated, and from one horizon to the next, there's only rust, the memory of a metal, and two frozen poles on opposite sides of the bed. What can't Mars forget? Night after night, you too must try to remember what heat is like. Again and again, you must search each other's bodies for the words of an old bolero. Look each other in the eye when you dance the Aided Suplex in the garden, or sing the Argentine Rack from the balcony, or strum the Samoan Drop in the veranda; hold hands when you undress your Russian Legsweep, your Battering Ram, your Double Bulldog Choke Slam. There will be nothing else, not even loss or victory, just time's perpetual spectacle. Kisses, punches—do everything as hard as you like. There is no dying on Mars, only Epimetheus. From the start, the match itself has been death, a moment always pointed backwards, and the longer you think about it (or the more you try to remember), it should be obvious that the afterlife has never been the future—but instead can only be the past. *Olé.*

Contrary to popular belief, the Sun and the Moon are actually equals embroiled in a longstanding game of brinkmanship. Look to the sky and you will see two bitter enemies of comparable size. Watch them chase each other, hurling endless threats. Watch them eclipse one another, taunting and braying. They put each other's lights out. They mimic the other's movement. In turn, they wave around the sky day and night, claiming all latitudes and longitudes as their own, like competing dogs pissing on every tree and bush in the forest. One's stink erases the other's, as it always has, and for you to have sex on either body, you must engage its enemy. These scales demand balance. Or else what? We need not find out. Serious sextronauts will allow themselves to become deadly weapons in an always escalating arms race between Helios and Selene. Word of your arrival on the Sun will be broadcast through secret channels and intercepted by unseen agents. Your lover's stationing on the Moon will be publicly alluded to but never officially recognized. All parties reserve plausible deniability. In alternating maneuvers, they will equip the two of you, following the pattern of a discrete function. One at a time and in taut rhythm, they will strip

147

you bare, smelt, and mold you. Gently, they will construct for you a propellant and a nozzle and then stuff you with powder. They'll gift you a monocoque structure, laced with vernier engines, gyroscopes, and gimbals. Back and forth, new accoutrements will be added as the stakes, following a von Neuman hierarchy, rise into absurdity. This is your courtship. A dangerous set theory that pits Hyperion plasma against Lunar modules. Staring at one another across 150 million miles of empty space, you and your lover will finally be launched in an interstellar game of chicken, a la Bertrand Russell, like two drunk teenagers on the edge of a cliff. Try to imagine it as fun. And keep drinking. Arcing through the void, you would do well to smile as you think of the Lagrangian Point—the place where the gravitational force between two bodies is equal—where the two of you can slow to a soothing stop and linger in the dark together forever. How nice. Yes, the time between discharge and inevitable impact should be just long enough for both of you to think of this stupid dream and to furiously rub one out while admitting to yourselves that you never actually thought of yourselves as equals—finally meeting in the middle at the intersection between A and B, a logical conjunction and pointless explosion. Then the Cold War continues without you.

2. The Middle and Outer Planets

Whereas the Inner Planets applaud personal choice and free will, sex farther out is definitively less casual. The next two subsections of the spheres constitute both order and disorder, rule and its subjugation, and they deftly establish how there is actually little difference in their dichotomies. So, the takeaway point here is that, obviously, the sex is going to be amazing. Of course, it goes without saying that it will also be out of this world. Beside our central star, the Middle Planets, Jupiter and Saturn, are the largest in the solar system, and, "Because of their enormous size, the regularity of their orbits, and the vast extent of their gravitational fields, they act like two great balance wheels to stabilize the system and keep celestial order in it."[1] And our Outer Planets—Uranus, Neptune, and the always contentious Pluto—are persona non grata presiding over rebellion, masochism, violence and delinquency. Allegiance to these bodies has historically been "rewarded with excommunication, imprisonment, death at the stake."[1] You may wish to establish a codeword, though ultimately it won't matter. It may be true that no one can hear you scream in space, but you're still going to. Now oil up.

Middle

At more than double the size of every other planet combined, Jupiter rests atop a great seat of power. It's well stocked, and there's no wonder that the most impressive Roman temple was built in its name. Jupiter's magnetosphere operates at a strength at least fourteen times that of Earth's. The attraction is uncontested, but be careful. Despite boasting a Jovial character, Jupiter is an unofficial police state, surrounded by a retinue of armed, icy moons. The Galilean satellites goosestep in tight, regular formation around its regal outer body, while the rocky core is shrouded beneath a blanket of gas and bureaucracy, mostly helium and earmarked legislation. Some interlopers suggest that the core doesn't even exist, like the king of Kafka's Castle or the unknown guard in the Panopticon prison, but it is this very uncertainty from which great power is drawn, striking fear in all comers. Central core or no, the enormous red eye watches over everything like an omniscient corner-deli camera. And as in the case of a bodega, it would be impossible to merely get down here and do it like dogs. You'd be ejected in an instant because of Jupiter's hold on both space and time. No, in order to fuck on Jupiter, or in a deli for that matter, one must emulate Zeus's rise to power, wherein he and his father fought as two bedbugs, the spearlike thunder cock of the one fiercely piercing the Titan carapace of the other, spilling rocks and Olympian children all over the heavens' filthy aisles. This traumatic insemination will, for better or worse, be the only sex on Jupiter. You must become an infestation of vermin spawning in its crannies, eluding incarceration in your sheer number and anarchy. You and your sleeper cells must fuck rampantly, in the breads and cereals, in the oatmeal and crackers, in the walls and the corners, in the frames and the linings, and you must do it with ferocity, without care for the other, in the name of a greater good, with idealism and hope: rape with a human face. It is in this manner that Jupiter truly wins, however, by eradicating the difference between revolution and rule, between Europa and the Bull. Here, all transgression of the law is a default affirmation. Your throng of bastard children will be absorbed into the shelves, and eventually you too will be sold and eaten. In a great reversal, you will have fucked and been fucked to no purpose, and your corruption will be of no solace or consequence to anyone. Attempts to call for justice will bring laughter and ridicule and character assassination, both for you and your family. Get on the floor and put your hands in the air. You're going to live.

On Saturn, it's always Saturday. A day of rest. A day of relaxation. A party that never stops. Saturnalia, the Golden Age, forever. Naked from perihelion to aphelion, with a cornucopia overflowing its horn of plenty, "Loose reins are given to public dissipation; everywhere you may hear the sound of great preparations."[3] Yes, sex is going to be easy. You'll leave your car keys on the outer rings and take off that blouse, kick off your boots and chillax while strangers casually have their way with you. It's nice. Everyone feels good and no one has to work. This is the great harvest! Yet, when the partiers go down on you, as if apathetically reading the Sunday paper, you'll realize that all this leisure is being dragged to an untenable conclusion, and the Sunday paper will never actually arrive. That cool breeze? Blows at 1,100 mph. That bowl of chips and dip? A massive, global storm, 12,000 miles across. Someone here is eating babies for fun. Someone has opened a vintage bottle of Furies, spilling both Eumenides, the kindly ones, and Erinyes, the angry ones, all over the shag carpet, and there is no stain remover on

Saturn. The sex doesn't stop. Sadly, permanent fellatio and cunnilingus are quickly becoming the true castration. There's cum everywhere and too much chafing. It smells like shit. For escape, you must invoke Saturn's patron angel, Cassiel. Use the amulet made in his name—intended to ward off enemies (your erstwhile lovers)—with words carved in the blood of a bird, tied to the legs of a dove, and set to flight. This should scatter the mob, yet the bird will not fly, and neither will your enemies. On Saturn, it's always Saturday, no matter the doves. What now? You can choose to further embrace Cassiel, to rest in passive judgement of the cosmos, staring with dead eyes over the bobbing heads of the endless parade of hysterical swingers—or you can become Shani, maleficent Navagraha of the Vedic texts, and dole out punishments, lopping the limbs off of kings, developing "systems of legal torture that function with cold, Saturnian efficiency,"[1] and embrace the soft melancholy that is so faithfully married to sadism, but either way you're staying at the party. So take a deep breath; it's going to be a long day.

Outer

It's logical that Uranus is the celestial haven of water sports and golden showers. Though English-speaking school children might protest otherwise, its name is drawn both from the Greek, *Fορσανος*, which is reminiscent of Sanskrit's "to rain," and more directly, *ουρEω*, meaning "to urinate." Some will wish to contradict these roots, boldly asserting that Uranus has cold feet, its temperature as low as -371°F. All of the unleashable liquid, they'll say, is frozen. And detractors will be quick to bring up the satellite Voyager's damning observation that Uranus is not pissing on anyone. Rather, they'll say, it stands just out of view with an axial tilt roughly parallel to that of the solar system itself, as if trying to blend shyly into the background. Skeptics will rightfully ask, if Uranus is one of only three gas giants and ruler of "revolution, crisis [and] reform,"[1] then why this prude inhibition? Admittedly, the specifics of its low thermal flux remain a scientific anomaly, and no, we cannot precisely explain its hydrocarbon haze layers, but the general cause of its inaction does not elude us. The reason? Not Uranus's symbolic relationship with castration, nor the fear of its own children, but the paraphilic act of Desperation—a.k.a., holding it in for sexual pleasure. Uranus isn't a prude—it's an unhinged voyeur getting off on this cold limbo. Uranus isn't hiding but lounging in a painful erotic repose. That's why it isn't peeing on anyone. And to have sex on Uranus, you too will have to embrace its philosophy. Don't try anything stupid, either: Uranus "responds to efforts to appease him... with intensified naughtiness, until finally his own personality becomes as diffuse, rootless, and lacking in direction as his causeless rebellion."[1] Sound familiar? Whether it does or doesn't, it should. Here, you must assent to the things you suppress. On Uranus, discover what is in your psychic bladder and make it stay there. Secrets ought to go unspoken, ambitions unrealized. Try to copulate and reproduce with the

153

idea of being alone, of never really accomplishing anything. More importantly, take pleasure in the sight of others doing the same. Watch them dance. Watch nothing happen until nothing reaches its fever pitch, where it doesn't shatter that wine glass, but threatens to. Anything is possible and it's staying that way—until everything is an assault, and waiting is battery. Or is it the reverse? Either way, if done correctly, it should hurt. Keep taking it, and feel the weight of the rest of your life push back. One more second. One more second. One more second. One more second. One more second. One more second. One more second.

Neptune's movement in Gustav Holst's The Planets is the only piece featuring human voices, a chorus of women hidden in a separate room from the audience. This illusion and chicanery is correspondent to the mystic planet's strange, almost magical promises. You will wonder: Who are these people, and what else is happening behind closed doors? Poseidon clouds the answers in fathomless ocean depths, yet he graciously invites you to dinner, dangling information before you—not to mention a trident of power, wealth, and love. To have sex here, you must accept, and why not? Like anyone else, you too want power, wealth and love, right? Wrong. Neptune is going to teach you what you really want. Neptune is going to show you what's behind those closed doors. After dinner, when you're thoroughly drunk, he will drag you under the water, bring you into the room, only to reveal that it is empty. "There's no one here," you will say, noticing for the first time the cheap rings that Neptune wears. "No," he will tell you, "it's not empty. You're here."[4] And then he'll close the door, leaving you to consider the cold, methane walls. But you will not be alone for long. Emerging from the scattered disc population and drunkenly tossing off their Kuiper Belt, resonant trans-Neptunians will refocus their gravity on you, repeatedly, as if trying to draw water from the furniture. Your payment? A constant supply of drugs and a few moments of broken sleep. After a fashion, you too will begin to sing. There are other rooms, you'll realize, with other people—the final chorus in Holst's symphony has always been a cry for help, calling over the harp and oboe to an unmoved citizenry. An unlikely hero will emerge, a new Martin Luther of the orchestral brothel: Neptune himself. He will champion your cause and demand your release, pointing out the names of his "cheap" planetary rings: Courage, Liberty, Equality and Fraternity. In his unlikely honor, you and your comrades will smash through the doors and onto the stage, halting the quintuple meter, making chaos of sheet music and stands, woodwinds and brass. You will set the timpani aflame and slaughter the string section. You will put the conductor against the wall, last words be damned. But these musicians are no wimps, either. They will muster their forces, garrison off the organ and blockade the first chairs. In a flurry of coattails and bow ties, they will launch a counterattack, push back your front, and cut off your supplies. Now, the real sex can begin. Held fast to the ground, a hand around your neck, you will turn your head to the audience and scream, pleading. But this has always been your part, your solo. Make them believe in magic, that live rabbits can really come from hats, and, rising from their seats, the guests will applaud you. It's been a fantastic show. Take a bow, if you can. Tomorrow, the performance starts again, almost everywhere, "until there is no difference between sound and silence." In rehearsal, Neptune will arrogantly wave his trident and whisper to you, "Stop pretending—this is what you've always wanted." If you sing loudly enough, maybe the part inside your body that he's right about will finally exit through your wide open mouth, like a live rabbit leaving a shallow hat.

Pluto, finally, floats alone on the edge of everything and oblivion without knowing who or what it is. For billions of years, it was nothing. Then, briefly, a planet. Now, after a symposium, a dwarf. Next? A worm? Who knows—its orbit is confused and unpredictable. Pluto stands between the solar system and eternity like Janus, god of doors. With two faces looking at once forward and back in time, Pluto as Janus represents both the dead in Hades's underworld and "the emergence of life-forms from the one-celled organism." The umbra, the darkest part of a shadow, is named for it, and "Pluto's weapon is the bomb," where "the unexploded... is a uterine symbol; the explosion is phallic."[1] The point? Pluto doesn't know where it ends and something else begins. Unfortunately then, your partner cannot accompany you to Pluto—because Pluto is both itself and its lover, as you must be here as well. You will practice autoerotic asphyxiation instead. Put the noose around your neck and let yourself go. As you get further from the sun, you will freeze like Pluto's atmosphere and fall toward the ground. Pluto's mass is even less than that of the moon's, so you will fall slowly, the noose uncoiling like cream sliding across a gently sloped table. Imagine the rope as a cord hooked up to a dialysis machine: "[She] tried to sleep during dialysis. Most of the time, she dreamt of herself on dialysis."[5] With your hand, stroke as the gambler does its poker machine: "I was gone. My body was there, outside the machine, but at the same time I was inside the machine... It's like playing against yourself—you are the machine; the machine is you."[6] Stay like this, hanging naked on the line between life and death, ascension and climax, orbit and universe, now and forever, like laundry in a breeze. Know that the solar wind is gradually blowing the surface of Pluto into space, one granule at a time. Let your memories rush out ahead of you, crossing through the umbra. What part of you do you want cast into the future? Then, at the end of your rope and in an immaculate conception, you will offer to the void the same two STDs granted you by God—one tenuous, the other infinite.

Bibliography

1.   Watters, Barbara. *Sex and the Outer Planets*. Valhalla Paperbacks, Ltd.: Washington, DC. 1971.

2.   Barthes, Roland. Translated by Lavers, Annette. *Mythologies*. Hill and Wang: New York, NY. 1972.

3.   Seneca. Epistle 18, 1-2.

4.   Morgan, Dolan in the voice of Neptune, Planet.

5.   Sanal, Aslihan. "The Dialysis Machine." *The Inner History of Devices*. Turkle, Sherry, Ed. MIT Press: Cambridge, MA. 2008.

6.   Schull, Natasha. "Video Poker." *The Inner History of Devices*. Turkle, Sherry, Ed. MIT Press: Cambridge, MA. 2008.

CELLS

Whereas I had just moments ago been gardening, now the gentleman, Don Pedro Imbroglio, held a knife to my throat. He needed information, and for one reason or another, felt certain I could provide it. I have a particular look about me perhaps, especially while weeding. Clearly, though, he was equally as certain I did not want to divulge anything—hence the knife. Yet, I did not have the information he wanted and I told him as much. The meaning of this confession, my lack of knowledge, was lost on Imbroglio, though, on account of him so strongly believing the first two suppositions: that I *did* have the information and I did not want to share it. Given these two "facts," obviously I would tell him that I didn't know anything. What other choice did I have? Yet, it was Imbroglio's intention to make very clear the choices—by pressing the blade hard against my throat, a trickle of blood soiling my shirt collar.

Considering the circumstances, I opted to give him the information he desired—despite the fact that I didn't actually have it. Again: what other choice did I have? Between death and a lie, it was an easy decision, and one I'd made many, many times before—I made it all up as I went along, telling him the fictitious names of important informers and agents, the invented whereabouts of certain, almost mythical, documents and files, and the overheard plans of impossible siege. Always I took care to fall short of expectations and at other times to offer far more than requested—for there is a rhythm and even an honesty to lying. The more I confessed, the clearer it became that, in spite of the knife, I alone held control of the situation.

162

I realized this because the pressure on my throat fluctuated not by the Don's whim, but according to the content of my confessions. Gold loosened the pressure, if only slightly, and any difficulties in obtaining gold would bring the knife closer. Yet, the solutions and pathways around these difficulties and obstacles brought the most relief from the blade, so I found myself constantly peppering my confession with gold, subsequently inhibiting the possibility of attaining it, and then generating elaborate but probable solutions. The knife waved in and out with each passing phrase, and soon I would discover the topic or phrase that simply lifted the knife away. Perhaps, even, there might be a word that makes a man turn the knife on himself. It was just a matter of time.

Second, I was in control because it was Imbroglio alone, not I, who would follow the instructions, trace the false paths

I prescribed—and essentially answer to my commands as if he were nothing but a dog. If the knife pulled away, I would go back about my business while Imbroglio left to slave over the complex, meaningless, and contradictory—even dangerous—directions I had laid out for him. Holding the knife to my throat, believing in its necessity, standing by its sharpness, Imbroglio had no other choice but to do exactly as I said.

It was a fine situation, so far as I was concerned, and it seemed to go on for quite some time. I continued to talk, offering increasingly fantastic information and suggesting ever more dangerous routes and chases. Yet, as safe and as powerful as I felt lying in the face of death, any observer would be quick to conclude I was in dire trouble, it being the case that a man had a knife to my throat. I could understand the confusion, but I was nevertheless irritated when a perfect stranger attempted to save me. My lies were just reaching a climactic vector—one involving a leap of faith, a golden chalice, and a gorge of crocodiles.

Yet the stranger emerged from the nearby shrubbery—perhaps having crawled there from a distance—and pounced toward Imbroglio. The stranger brandished his own knife and held it to Don Pedro Imbroglio's throat. "Stand down," he demanded, his mustache atwitter. My irritation turned to fascination, however, as the man continued, naming my own attacker: "Don Pedro, you have some information that I need." He was neither a stranger nor a savior, but a soldier.

Of course, Don Pedro claimed not to know anything—but the new man, Masaro, deduced the *very same false conclusion* that Don Pedro had come to about me: that Don Pedro knew everything, in fact, but simply *did not want* to share it. The knife pressed ever harder on Imbroglio's throat, and believing just as much as Don Pedro in the truth-charging properties of the blade, Masaro incessantly requested information—the very same information in fact that Don Pedro had asked of me. Yet, remarkably, when Don Pedro Imbroglio caved, gave in and agreed to answer the questions—his neck streaked with small droplets of blood—the Don did not impart the information I had just moments ago given him, but invented wholly other fantastical and dangerous leads, as if in an attempt to control the knife of Masaro.

164   I began to get nervous watching the knife bob up and down against Imbroglio's throat, loosening and tightening with the stories Imbroglio told. How long would it be before the Don noted that if *he* could sway the pressure of death with his lies, why couldn't I? I watched the movements of his face for any trace of realization or angered epiphany. Before he could put it all together, however, from behind a rock jumped a new man, calling Masaro's name and unsheathing a stubby sword. He pressed it against Masaro's throat.

Another man come for the information? No, I was mistaken: the new man asked for no information, but instead bellowed, "Let go of my comrade Don Pedro or I will gut you like a fat fish." And with that declaration he pushed hard into Masaro's neck with the blade—and Masaro retaliated in turn by pressing harder upon Don Pedro Imbroglio's neck, and thus, as if out of politeness or good manners, Don Pedro pushed his blade harder into *my* neck. This movement of force from one person to the other suffered the four of us to begin to rotate, thus lessening the pressure on our throats ever so slightly, the knives having to follow just behind our twisting course.

Spinning there in my garden, we trampled over the flowers, crushing them *and* a season's worth of work—while the three other men, Don Pedro Imbroglio, Masaro, and the new man, Genaro, argued over information and honor. Depending on who was speaking directly to whom, the pressure of the blades varied from throat to throat. The only exception was that Don Pedro kept a constant hold on mine, never wavering, and I moved backwards to compensate, ensuring our constant rotation, each one of them circling around after me. Yet, while Genaro spoke to Masaro of gutting him, Masaro's neck felt the most pain—and Masaro therefore moved the most, exerting the greatest influence on our small circle's rotation, *pushing it and all of us slightly to the right.* And though Masaro might turn to Don Pedro, demand information angrily, and think himself in control by drawing blood from Imbroglio's neck, Imbroglio—or whoever was most attacked, whoever was closest to death, whoever had the sharpest reason to move—would exert the firmest control over where our rotation took us in the garden.

165

Meanwhile, I could see just across the garden a set of shears, only just recently sharpened for spring maintenance, and I made it my intention to influence the conversation such that our rotating knife entanglement might move in the direction of the tool. It was a delicate process because it required that I speak in a manner that would infuriate the man *next* to that which I intended to control—that is, if I wanted Masaro to push the rotating circle to the right, I would have to mention something to *Genaro* that made him press the knife hard on the soldier's throat, thus allowing Masaro to exert, out of fear, the most influence over our direction. And to get Don Pedro to move the circle, I had to offer information to Masaro that made *him* close in on the Don.

And because we were constantly turning, the gardening shears kept changing place in reference to the four of us—as if the garden itself were spinning. Thus, I changed who I spoke to quite often, trying to give control to whoever was lined up with my gardening shears as they spun around us. It was indeed slow going, but eventually I was within reach of the shears. I snatched them up into my hand and placed them at Genaro's throat. And so there we all were, completely balanced, each one a victim and an attacker, while the world spun around us.

We went on like that for some time. Or the garden did.

It quickly became hard to tell what was moving and what wasn't. That is, now that we were even, the blades and necks equally balanced, it was impossible to tell who was moving what, who was pushing where, or if anyone was moving at all. Try as I might to influence our direction through purposeful conversation, all motion seemed random—be it the garden's or our own. The only certainty we had was that we could all in turn kill each other. Soon, as well, it also became clear that the others knew just as much as me, that they had come to the same realizations. Masaro would tell stories that intentionally angered the men next to me, Genaro and Don Pedro, and would then grimace when I failed to lead the motion of our circle. The trick wasn't working anymore. Everyone told stories and everyone was disappointed at the results, the circle moving across the garden chaotically and without course. We had no choice but to move with it, the blades guiding each one of us.

Everyone kept their weapon at the next one's neck, for who ever took it down would be at a disadvantage. Yet, so long as we all kept on this way, we were trapped in the circle with each other having, despite our knives, no control over where we went. In effect, we relinquished control in order to stay in control and had no choice but to have no choice.

My wife poked her head out of the kitchen window, looked into the garden and asked, "What are you doing out there?"

"I'm not so sure," I replied, "And actually I have no idea—what does it look like from there? What are we doing?"

"Well, I don't know why you would be—with all this work that needs doing—but from what I can tell, I think you all are heading over there toward the fence."

She was right: the chaotic course of our rotating blade entanglement had made a sudden but plaintive move toward the wooden fence, the one I had been meaning to fix. At first cautious, the motion became *intent and uninhibited*— our circle was making its way along the garden path with

167

speed and precision. I went over the possibilities again and again, but I could not pinpoint which one of us was making it happen. We all fell silent, the stories and demands coming to a halt, *but the circle kept moving.*

We kept moving. It kept moving.

Our blade-knot twirled through the garden, over the yard, and into the street. My wife called something out in protest but the circle moved away too quickly for us to catch what she said. Besides, we were all transfixed by the movement none of us was planning, the movement of the circle in which we were trapped. Spinning past the houses, it reached an intersection, stopped for a moment, and then made a deliberate left toward the market. We traipsed up to the fruit stand, where fat old Marco sat idly reading and swatting flies, then barreled intentionally, or at least precisely, through the apples and pears, and moved on toward the rug hut. Marco called out to us as we spun around the carts and the displays, but our circle, our ring of blades and demands, wanted neither apples nor rugs. Deftly maneuvering we twirled through the crowd, artfully dodging across the town on into the pastures—searching for whatever the four of us together wanted more than any one of us individually. Or just as much—for the circle only moved at the behest of our own unfulfilled interests here inside.

In a field just outside town, our circle moved deliberately from one cow to the next as if inspecting them, making clear straight lines after long and thoughtful pauses. What did we or it want from the cows? It was beyond me for

168

sure. Throughout, we told stories to each other, still futilely attempting to influence our direction—mostly out of habit. With time our stories became less antagonistic and more nostalgic, increasingly fueled by a hidden camaraderie. Don Pedro had once owned a bookshop. Masaro loved a woman across the sea and Genaro was a prize-winning horse racer. And on we plodded, searching for something we could never guess or understand we were looking for.

Soon, though, we weren't the only ones jostling about the fields: across the way another group of spinning violence struck a path around the cows. These men had each other with guns to the head, arguing over who knows what. Occasionally we came within hearing distance or even touching distance, but we never interacted. After a spell, there was another circle, then another, and then another, until the field was brimming with almost everyone in the town. The dentist held a drill against the head of a child who aimed a sling shot at the face of the pastor who waved a small dagger around the gut of a woman with a miniature revolver—and they conversed almost casually, holding death just out of sight.

While recalling a memory of her, I saw my mother holding a gun to a man's head, spinning past us. As I spoke of her, it was as if from a dream, an old book I read once long ago. We saw everyone we knew there, but only glimpses. It could never be more with all the motion there in the field. And as we spun, it seemed our own circle befriended a few circles nearby—thus around a cow a circle of circles formed.

None of us were surprised when we started floating into

169

the air. Not that I didn't note its strangeness—I certainly did, and I'm sure we all did, but not so much as to break the chain of blades and information. With all of the town floating in the air above the cow pasture, spinning and twirling, groups began to form and enlarge. Soon, it was apparent that the lot of us had created one large unit, singular though bloblike. We moved forward in unison, all of us, as one and with intent. And the blob of our town met another town's blob, and then many blobs. And they spun about until we were a part of something much larger—and what else could we do down here but tell each other stories of things that maybe we were doing up there? We weren't about to lay aside our weapons, that's for sure. We speculated on the nature of what we might be aiming for, all of us together, but it was just guesswork.

170

We floated through rivers of people, all jostling about, and surmised that perhaps we were on our way to somewhere important. We also recalled where we had come from, wondering whether or not it was just as fanciful as our speculations about the future. Had I really been a gardener? Had Masaro ever fought in the war? Was Don Pedro Imbroglio's sister really a cripple? Had Genaro ever bathed in the ocean? We told so many stories, it was hard to remember. I recalled or imagined that at one time I had known or believed or bluffed that deep within the plants I had tended and the flowers I had watered, there were whispered lies and fantasies holding everything together. Masaro recalled or invented a time when he had taught or misled a friend: "Everything in our bodies has something else in mind." And Genaro and

Don Pedro agreed that it may or may not have been true that they had pulled in opposite directions but brought something to the same place. And together we imagined or deduced that the stars never moved because they feared each other. Just as much, though, we lied or insisted that none of these things were true, but rather, it was how the plants and the stars and our bodies and things felt or dreamed about us.

Every now and then, too, as if to remind each other of our own intentions, while we floated into the air, spinning in a cloud of spinning people in a blob of twirling clouds in a twirling something-we-could-never-know, Masaro or Don Pedro Imbroglio would demand the information they came for originally, but no one took them seriously, and it was as if it was all just a silly joke. The things you've always wanted— *haha*. An elbow to the ribs. The intentions of the circle, of everything around us, our combined interests, we took more seriously, perhaps only because we could not understand them. Still, God help whatever it is, this thing we are a part of, if anyone down here gets the answers they sought so long ago, if any one ever gets what they want.

That's when the knives come down.

INVESTMENT BANKING
IN REVERSE

Hundreds of umbrellas call for serious protection, not just a lock or bolt or curtain. Look at them there, all black and open, scattered across the roofless warehouse floor—so vulnerable. They needed me. What would they be without me? Just another heap of forgotten ideas fluttering about a dying fire, some meaningless amalgamation of chemical, alloy, and fabric. I could give them more than protection—definition, purpose, direction and utility. Where the building once met the ceiling, hills of shattered brick and dust filtered the sunlight into distinct rays, thick beams that fell hard on the sea of umbrellas—as if the elements aimed to destroy them all, one by one, were it not for my stewardship. I'd counted the lucky find fifty times or more, spending the afternoon traipsing through the warehouse, back and forth, smiling and not believing it to be real: four hundred thirty-two black-nylon-fiberglass-and-aluminum-retractable-oak-handled umbrellas. All mine—all my flock of motionless, rain-resistant sheep.

But how to keep them safe?

Outside the splintered warehouse doors, the dry earth's cracks and fractures spun toward the business center's main drag, still clouded in gusts of wind and dust that raced casually around occasional, jutting remnants of industry. Here and there, forklifts sat naked where businesses used to open and close. Unrecognizable machines and appliances waited for someone to use them, desk chairs called out to be sat on, tangled phones impatiently strangled loose, unread files— but no one came here anymore. The storms and sadness and fear of radiators kept us out. Of course, other people passed through the business center, but not for long and not from our town. Our town sat safely over the hill and in the valley, everyone *"LOOKING FORWARD, NOT BACK!"* with a current of unspoken *"PLEASE DON'T REMIND ME WHAT'S HAPPENING"* that always threatened to make the transition to spoken but never realized it. My father told me visiting the business center is nostalgic, sentimental and naive. Years ago, he worked here, commuting every day by train. What once took him just a half hour now exhausted over an hour and a half of my morning and afternoon, a rocky bike ride in both directions. I hoped the isolation might protect the umbrellas from would-be entrepreneurs, if only until I thought of something more secure, but time was short.

Apprehension seized me and I had to stop and look back just one more time before I left my umbrellas behind. God, they were glorious! I made fists and danced, then hopped on my bike and pedaled off over the foundations of forgotten stores and shops, shielding my eyes from the dirt, practically singing. Maybe I could revitalize the area with my booming weather preparation business! "Sure, we started small, but you can never get enough umbrellas—that's my motto," I'd tell the reporters. In any case, I could get a leg up on my loans. Maybe at this year's Loan Day Celebration the town council would crown me with the plastic scepter and ceremonial sash so that I could lord it over everyone while we snacked on peaches and fruit cups. Me—King of the Loans! For a day! Or an evening, rather, but still, I could just about taste all of the three to four hours of glory, syrupy sweet.

I pedaled into town through the old turkey path, dodging cans and bones and old newspaper, skidded out onto Park Street and made my way to the bus stop, barely able to hold in my giddy mood. Collin waited for me on the bench. He almost made the place look like a bus could show up, if you covered one eye and pretended the sign that said *NO BUSES* meant something else. In a way it did, but not anything I ever understood. I put on my best "I haven't been ecstatic about four hundred thirty-two umbrellas" pose when I approached him. It included at least 20% glower, but also equal parts tousled hair and hand in the pocket. "What are you so happy about?" Collin asked without even looking at me. He had a fish in a bucket next to his feet that splashed and flapped like flapping and splashing might make a difference. The hook fresh in its mouth leaked cloudy wisps of pale blood, pink in the grey water.

"Nothing, why do you ask?"

He shrugged his shoulders and did that thing where he looks off into the distance because he wants to say something but can't figure out how yet. I sat down next to him on the bench and we both gazed toward the mountains. I took out some sliced mango from my pack and started eating it. Collin had some too. He sighed and tapped his fingers. "So," struggling to find the words, he squinted a bit and then said, "we have to go to the post office because your dad agreed to bare-knuckle box Carl Stanley for everything he owns there in the back lot and everyone's going to be there and man, I'm sorry I had to be the one to tell you but there it is so let's go because we're probably already late." I chewed my mango, then another slice. Not quite ripe.

The post office roof held hundreds of onlookers, but Collin and I managed to squeeze to the front. Down below, a circle of locals and postmen caged my dad and Clark, both bloody and shirtless. Mr. Stanley didn't need to box my dad, but debt collectors usually agree if you ask. Ever since the issuing of our new interest rate contracts, which included "the boxing clause," basically a cruel joke I think, stating that "any persons in a fiscal relationship with Sally May Holdings, Inc. can, if they choose to do so, file for a boxing match, pursuant of a claim to paid-in-full standing, to be witnessed and refereed by officials of the collector's choosing, and following standard bare-knuckle regulations and procedures," upstanding men opted to lose everything on a bout of fists they couldn't win. Each one of them believed that they, finally, would triumph as the single hero to beat the mountain, but debt collectors are well fed, well trained, and have the refs on their side, so it's all hopeless. But if anyone could do it, my dad could.

He didn't though. Mr. Stanley's chest dripped blood, but not an ounce of his own. He pounded my father like an angry baker kneading bread. For a moment it looked as if my father had reached into himself and found the secret, the hate, the drive and the love and the hope to bury Mr. Stanley under a maelstrom of new strength that can only come from near defeat, but the secret ended up just being a gurgle of teeth and blood and spit and dirt, all the ingredients of every myth and fable of the have-nots, dripping off his chin and waiting for a silver spoon. My dad didn't look like a hero, but more like an undercooked calzone flopped in a heap on the post office tarmac. Mr. Stanley toweled off his immense body and I told Collin I needed his help.

"With what?" he asked.

"Security," I said. "And umbrellas."

I didn't say anything else until much later that night. First I saw to my father's emergency medical care, assured his smooth admittance to the hospital, the last of my paycheck incrementally exchanging a glove shop's worth of hands. Dad had been taking out Mr. Cormack's trash for a few months, so I handled that in his stead. Most of the lawns in the area are well maintained, but Mr. Cormack's is immaculate—lush, lizard green and a cool, tender texture. If he didn't have the energy to remove the trash, I can only guess where the strength to comb over the lawn could have come from. Or maybe he just didn't have time for the trash, his dedication overriding

177

responsibility and hygiene. Whenever I accompanied Dad to Mr. Cormack's house, we'd find him either hunched over a patch of weeds visible only to him or silently slouched on his porch chair in an argyle sweater, drinking canned iced tea, his face a haphazard muddle of raw chicken and gristle. He smiled, though, like there was nothing better in the world than canned iced tea and argyle.

Convincing Collin to come with me into the business center didn't prove easy, but he agreed one shaky step at a time until finally the warehouse loomed over us that night, its secret and fantastic contents waiting for protection. We established that, given I had discovered the umbrellas in the first place, I would receive the direct profits and that Collin had been taken on simply as a temporary employee and not a primary stakeholder and therefore he should be paid accordingly. That out of the way, we began security enhancements. First we decided to move the umbrellas into a safer location. A basement filled with holiday cards and decorations and tissue paper would do. Once each umbrella had been transported, counted and then recounted, we stacked boxes of stationary at the foot of the basement stairs, then placed a spare door from a nearby office skeleton over the entrance, and topped it all off with some loose shrubbery, nothing fancy but enough to keep the place from drawing attention to itself. We didn't want any random nomads wandering accidently upon our horde. Next, we waited for the rainy season to approach. I figured the best time for attack would be when other umbrellas sold at much higher rates. While competitors tried to cash in on increased need, we could swoop in and sell at unbeatable prices because it amounted to pure profit for us. Our competitors, mainly John Roebuck and his some fifteen rental umbrellas or Sarah Contwin and her plastic rain hoodies, wouldn't know what hit them when our cheap and magically stylish umbrellas suddenly flooded the town. With any luck, Dad and I could get ourselves out of default and back on regular payments.

I spent the rest of the summer visiting Dad at the hospital in the morning, cycling out to count my umbrellas, working afternoons at the credit processing mill, occasionally removing Mr. Cormack's trash, and enjoying the night on my own. Dad's stay at the hospital shouldn't have been so long, all his wounds healed in a week, but since he had taken time off work to recuperate and didn't want to fall any further behind on his payments, he entered into an experimental drug and procedure program, allowing the doctors to test what they remembered of remedies on him, remedies and memories that usually ended up extending his stay on the grounds of this or that side effect or, more often, mistake or lapse of foresight— which in turn prompted him to re-enroll into the testing, on and on until months had passed and the doctors grappled with the fact that maybe they'd never remember. His face like a rotted eggplant, bloated with everything the doctor's had incorrectly recalled, Dad swore he had a plan, that his hospital bank accounts amassed funds and interest with every new drug and donated organ, with every spark of medical déjà vu, but he and I both knew I had access to the accounts and not only were they not amassing funds or interest, but they were deep in the red because he'd been paying his bills on hospital credit coins—which could only be purchased in exchange for increased APR on his outstanding college loans. Once, while he slept, I found his stash of bloody tissues in the plastic drawer by his cot, filled with black chunks and mushy pieces of his lungs or throat. So, these are memories, I thought. I never mentioned it, just left, making sure to smile and wave to Mr. Stanley, honorary chair of hospital proceedings.

Nights, I sat in the bus stop fiddling with my half deck of cards and listening to the credit mill's clanking and buzzing. Soon things would be different, I thought. Lounging with my back against old advertisements for movies I'd never see, I put my feet up on a crate, stared out toward the fog and stars resting over the mountains and the restored steamboat in the river, my pants wet with dew, and imagined myself shouting orders from a desk to my many umbrella employees, all of whom delighted in keeping the world dry. Sometimes Collin joined me. Other times, he didn't. Sometimes we talked. Other times, we didn't. Silent or chatting, we didn't come to the bus stop for conversation, but just to watch things not happen, to not see buses arrive, to not watch people commute, to not hear the news or gossip or facts, but to listen to the dragonflies sleeping on the edge of the stream, to watch restless birds finally settle in dead lime trees.

The first trickle of rain hit my cheeks at the September Bazaar. The Credit Mill sponsored it every year and I'd just been promoted to litter removal, so I had access to everything because people leave trash even, and especially, in the most exclusive of places. I made my way around the rugs covered in half-price memories—records no one could listen to, appliances that couldn't work, unused tickets to shows that never happened and never would, photos of places that no longer existed, dead batteries—little pieces of the lives we'd planned to live, passed and traded among us until, one by one, we'd eventually all not live the very same life, having held or owned the same trinkets of the past, if only for a brief time, if only to resell it to the next person. The Bazaar didn't give us anything new really, mostly just a chance, if we couldn't finish our own lives the way we'd anticipated, to partake in what was left of everyone else's. Still, a few sold makeshift impersonations of the things we'd once enjoyed or needed: wobbly handmade candles, "designer" curtains sewn from found sheets and shirts, cardboard cribs, and caustic, tub brewed soaps, though no one made any money really, just moved it around from here to there. John Roebuck and Sarah Contwin manned their well-established stalls, business gaining reasonable speed with the thickening clouds, enough at least for them to buy a few things or make a daily payment to Sally May. As it began to pour, I cornered Collin while he manned a special exhibit from the Credit Mill, a collection of photos from the top of a building in a city no one could remember but said they did, and I told him to prepare for opening day, that the great umbrella sale begins tomorrow.

At the close of the Bazaar, I sat and listened to Father Raymark, introduced by Mr. Stanley, giving a speech about our innate greatness, our wondrous lineage, the same one he recited every year under the banner that read, *AUTO SHOW: SEPT 16TH!*, the only banner we had, tattered and patchy blue. He reminded us that 6,000 years ago, Adam and Eve had been expelled from their homeland, not in the same way we had, really, because maybe our homeland had been more expelled from us, poof just like that, but either way we'd been separated from it all the same, and like us, they too had a debt to pay, a debt to God, a debt that over time, generation by generation their bloodline should have paid off in full but never did in their wicked hearts, and their spiritual accounts dwindled and dwindled until nothing was left and the only thing God could do was purge the earth once again in fire and confusion, cutting his losses, and though that debt has bankrupted, Father Raymark said, though we come from incompetent stock of inept Abrahams and negligent Mohammeds, we, the new Adams and Eves, could overcome and be the final lineage that establishes a good line of credit with the Lord our God Amen, who in his grace left but one institution standing, the great vein that leads up to the heavens, the collection agencies whose ministers are strong and righteous, who still believe in us and make our case to the Lord though they needn't but just out of the goodness of their huge hearts, you see, until one day our children's children's children will live debt free in a paradise of flowing commerce and renewed consumerism baptized in a tide of everything we could hope for and more and thank you very much for attending the bazaar, we'll see you next year. As Mr. Stanley clapped, so did we. I didn't go in for religion so much, but the basics were there and not so far off base anyway. I owed somebody money for my dad's social work degree, whoever it was, mortal or God, that much was clear.

Collin and I spent the night loading and carting our umbrellas out of the business district and back to town. The rain had stopped, and out there in the dark you'd catch glimpses of lizards skittering around rocks and stray bricks. The moon cast shadows like thin blankets over the dirt and patches of damp sidewalk. Somewhere, my mother, who'd been claimed by the Sally May company under the rules of eminent domain, was looking at the same moon or maybe a nice picture of it or a wall or a man's strained face or abdomen I guessed. Collin, whose mum had become akin to a sort of company drinking fountain, an honor according to Mr. Stanley, said it's best not to think about it too much. He's right. If you think about anything too long, you lose precious time, time you could be packing umbrellas onto a cart on the back of a bike in the middle of the night under the moon with lizards.

We slept with our product under a tree in the middle of town, half rotted limes under and around us. In the morning, we climbed its branches and hung the umbrellas like enormous black fruit, the dying tree ripened and blooming with our sales tactics. It was sunny and cloudless, but everything still dripped from last night's rain, a hot steam rising with the sun, and once people awoke, sales were immediate and fantastic. We sold ten umbrellas! And another six the next day. My finances ballooned twice over within a week and I managed to balance dad's hospital account, telling him to lay low and let his nails grow back without enrolling in any new programs. By the end of September, rain pushing streams up over their banks, I was two months ahead in my loan payments and wearing newish shoes. Both Mr. Stanley and Father Raymark shook my hand and congratulated me when I started a savings account, one of four in the town.

So, obviously, after the town council illegalized umbrellas, I wasn't very happy. Even if I could have sold them on the sly, no one had a reason to buy if they couldn't be seen in town with them. Joe Roebuck and Sarah Contwin beamed with energy as they potted around neighborhoods stealing back all of my customers and hawking their mediocre wares— which somehow skirted the classification of umbrellas in a suspicious technicality—while Mr. Stanley gave out a small reward to every person who dropped an umbrella off at the Credit Mill. Collin and I aimed to make the best of it. Though the act made me sad in a way, as if I had failed them somehow, as if I hadn't protected them like I had sworn or been born to, as if in finding them I had ushered them into disutility faster than nature intended, still we took two garbage bins from the rec hall in the middle of the night, stole off to the business center, gathered up every last umbrella, dragged them back to town through a shower of wet, tired pedals, and, come morning, loped up the hill, busted into the Credit Mill, pushed our way through the workers to Mr. Stanley's office, requested an audience and dumped our one hundred umbrellas out across the studio floor, demanding our due reward for our triumph of civic duty. We were promptly arrested and charged six months advance payments, double interest. While we were incarcerated, the town council stamped the umbrellas with an official seal, deemed them safe for regular use, and resold them at marked up prices just in time for the late autumn torrents.

Prison isn't so bad except that you can't work. There's food and a place to sleep, good company, but everyone is miserable knowing that those numbers multiply and appreciate with each day in lock up, no matter how well we eat or rest. Collin stopped talking to me and disappeared into a haze of strangers. There was a Sally May sighting in the shower and Father Raymark came to officiate it wearing a pair of dark, somber sunglasses "to cast off the lesser light, to better see the image of our lady," an image that in fact resembled more a pigeon than a benefactor and really, obviously, just some rust and mildew, dripping soap scum—and besides which Father Raymark smelled of whiskey and gin. He took me aside and told me that something called DNA lived inside me and that whatever schemes I might plan I couldn't avoid the payment, real and honest, because the final ledger of my accounts was scrawled by God in an immense code that every cell of my body contained. I knew all this already, of course. I'd been born with it, he said, putting his hand on my shoulder, and I would die with it too, but if I wanted to improve the code through righteous will and to pass on a biological ledger a father could be proud of, then the path was clear. Not until my release from the jail and the discovery of my father's death, an assisted suicide, and his body's subsequent donation to the hospital, slated as compensation for another account he'd kept hidden from me, an account that he'd tried to fill with the money from multiple experiments and tests and drugs but that he'd only emptied and depleted deeper and deeper until the numbers no longer made any sense at all but instead seemed to infect you with their very existence, and the doctor's deemed it best that he be in the care of scientists because probably his body, with its so bankrupt a genetic code, could very well contaminate the soil and present a terrible risk to all of us, and all went as planned until Mr. Stanley intervened and confiscated the body, claiming my father as a saint and a martyr, a man who did not commit suicide but died destroying his body to protect and improve the accounts of his bloodline and that, though he may have failed in the end and pitifully so, still he was a hero because perhaps his final act was to protect his credit line from himself, a degenerate and incompetent man, which in turn made him, finally, a hero and one who deserved nothing better than a proper burial outside the Credit Mill and wouldn't his son honor his noble father with a eulogy?, and everyone smiled and everyone clapped and patted me on the back with tears in their eyes—only then did I realize the truth in Father Raymark's words, that the path was very clear, and so I filed for a bare-knuckle boxing match with Clark Stanley the following day.

186

I took out Mr. Cormack's trash that evening, though he had very little of it.

In the early afternoon, a crowd gathered in the back lot

of the post office, everyone excited to see a young man bleed. As they breathed deeply, huddled and mashed together, placing bets and keeping a circle open for the fight to occur, Mr. Stanley casually played checkers with himself atop a sideways crate. And while they all enjoyed the hours off from work, complimentary whenever a boxing match is scheduled, though not a respite from compounding interest, I smashed through a window in every home, took off one by one with their umbrellas, made my final stop at the Credit Mill and reclaimed my shivering flock, then shepherded them all along with me into the business center, safe under the cover of a sandstorm and headed for nowhere in particular. The common notion around town had been that where we lived existed as an unlikely haven in a desert of danger, uncertainty, grief, and death. By venturing boldly into the business center, without the intention of returning but instead of seeking out what lay beyond, those I'd left behind surely considered me as good as dead, another suicide, just like my father's, though far more cowardly and much less laudable. No burials for me, no sainthood or martyrdom, not even a donation to science.

After a nominal stretch of dry, aggressive earth, the landscape became surprisingly docile, soft and green. In more remote places, airplanes, or pieces of them, scattered open areas. Lengths of road sometimes emerged from the dirt like lights in fog, receding again into the ground or the air or nothing, like the weather itself. For some time, I hoped to look back to find Collin enlarging like a speck of pepper into the shape of a man, but the only thing behind me was a waving haze obscuring the thin line between the sky and the earth. I spent a long time walking an old highway, useless radio and cell phone towers revealed on the periphery, lonely stalks of celery in an empty bed of concrete lettuce. Eventually, outposts became more frequent, usually lone homes on fields of foundations where a family or hermit or runaway would trade at least something for an umbrella, sometimes food or water, other times can openers and pans or shoes. After a time, I ran out of umbrellas, fulfilling my debt to their utility, but leaving me stupidly lonely. I didn't miss people anymore, but things.

Weeks later, an empty but otherwise intact town appeared over a bridge early in the morning. Lime and mango trees grew in the yards, young and virile, pulsating with juice. I strode about its clean streets under unlighted streetlamps and perused the homes as if picking produce in a grocery aisle. I plucked two for good measure and struck up a routine of living on and off in both, one small and unassuming, the other larger and ornate, gaudy paintings hanging crooked on the walls. Other people came, too, slowly and often in the night. I'd wake up and there'd be more neighbors, families tending lawns and repairing shutters as if they'd always been there, like it was just spring cleaning after a long winter. Eventually, I had to relegate myself to just one home, the smaller of the two, making way for three families willing to share the gaudy paintings and endless rooms.

I always half expected Mr. Stanley to come find me,

to send his agents and salesmen in search of me, valuable capital to be retaken. I imagined that I'd peer out my blinds to see suited men in sunglasses, or fat putty-faced men in stubby ties and brown shoes finally cornering me, but Mr. Stanley didn't need to send anyone. He came in the form of development and change and culture and commerce, in roads and infrastructure, transport and communication, unions and schools and celebrations. He never reached out, the world just got smaller, his hands waiting patiently for their mass to attract me. As usual, Eden inflated, exile waned, and my old accounts arrived by special post delivery in the weekend mail, only a few months after I'd started receiving it at all. I sat with the envelope on a rock outside my home, and I didn't even open it or the next one or the next one or any one, just let the interest rise like yeast in the oven, let the numbers assemble like blood cells from marrow—because what else is a balanced account but death? This way, I could live forever, I thought, in default—because debt doesn't die, it mails itself around our bodies and roads, getting bigger and bigger. My father's shrunken frame before his death—and those enormous and horrifying numbers practically pulsing off the ledger, daunting and awing, there was something in all that, a connection at least, and I think much more. So I let them grow, my numbers, let them increase and scatter and pepper banks and offices and papers, because maybe, like a tree giving its final fruit, paying it off is the real exile.

189

NUÉE ARDENTE

On the train ride north, I see an explosion in the distance. Black smoke rises into the afternoon sky, and I watch it out the window as the train speeds through tiny, blue-collar towns. The tower of smoke is like a building, a distant skyscraper that curves without care. The mountains beneath it seem almost uninhabited, covered in a thick rug of frosted pines. What's happening over there, I wonder. A forest fire? An industrial accident? A dormant volcano that has suddenly awoken? The landscape is unfazed. Still, I imagine all the mountains bursting open like bottles of cheap champagne—*pop, pop, pop*—covering the northern New York countryside with molten rock, washing over small towns with magma and steam, trailing smoke across the Eastern seaboard. The whole area will come to a stop once the 60 mph pyroclastic wave rolls down the hillsides and into town, I think. Like Pompeii, everyone will be halted in their tracks—and no matter what they were doing, be it humiliating or heroic or mundane, it will all be frozen here in the upstate territories like an enormous carbon photograph stretching the length of the Catskills. Soon it might become a sort of solemn tourist attraction like that of the World Trade Center or Pearl Harbor. People will come to witness tragedy firsthand, to see everything as it was "that terrible day." After a while, the shock and sadness of it all will most likely wear off, as if tragedy were just a perfume or cologne or bug spray you applied at the right moment, and people will come unabashed to look at all the privacies left behind and unguarded. No one will pay attention to its enormity, of course, or at least only pay it lip service, but everyone will string along their families to be voyeurs of the dead, standing their children in front of copulating corpses and taking photographs to be hung on the wall at home. At any given time, I realize, I probably would rather not have a volcanic plume rush over me and immortalize whatever it was I was doing at the moment. There are very few points in my life that I would choose to showcase as a tourist attraction, simply because most of the time I look like an idiot. Right now, for example: I'm slumped against the train window, my cheek stretched against the glass like putty. I probably resemble a puffer fish as it's prepared by a chef to be eaten: confused and asphyxiated.

Yet I'm breathing and fairly cognizant. In an hour, the train will pull into Binghamton, where my sister will meet me at the station. She'll be driving some beater that needs a screw driver shoved in the ignition to get it started, rust about to eat through the axles, and one window made of plastic garbage bags duct-taped gingerly to the frame. We'll zip along dirt roads for an hour until we reach her trailer on the top of a hill where we will eat hot dogs with her children, surrounded by jars of everything from pickled cabbage to pickled nuts. It's been years since I've seen her, but I know what to expect. And the years passed aren't because of a falling out or any kind of drama at all; simply, we've been busy—or I have—or just as much, we've never been close enough to warrant the expensive commute between NYC and the Canadian border. She's much older than me, a decade at least, and I sometimes have trouble seeing myself in her. She has said to our mother that we are oil and water, nothing alike and not worth comparing. It might be all we agree on, in fact. Really, everything else is so foreign to me, just as I imagine my life must be to her. The city, the noise, the fast pace—it's nothing like what she has sought and found. And how she came to living out here in the backwoods of America, in the middle of nowhere? I can't understand it. What does she find out here all alone? Maybe the cold: the area is known for its harsh winters—sometimes more than eight to ten feet of snowfall—which, unbelievably, leaves people even more removed than they already are from each other. I suppose, though, if you come for the isolation, then the winter snowdrifts aren't all bad. Luckily for me, it's November and that isn't winter in my book. The train speeds onward, now curving around a lake and giving me a better view of the smoke. It appears that there might be another cloud rising, but I can't tell if it's just another part of the first. I haven't heard any other explosions, but we are a great deal

193

farther off by now as well.

The sound of the train rushing along the steel tracks is suddenly audible as a woman whom I had seen earlier boarding the train drags her bags through my car and into the next. I recognize her as someone I may have known or been associated with, if only slightly, maybe an old college classmate or subway rider. I know her, I think. Still, she is familiar, just as much, as the type of girl that exists as a ghost in my head, the woman who seems like some perfect ideal— but whose parts are strewn across the bodies of millions of women, some limbs and smiles here, some eyes or clothes over here, and attitudes and laughs over there. The platform woman's snarly, sharp-toothed smile is a smile taken straight from the ghost's blueprint. Her eyes and legs seem familiar too, as if they were somewhere inside me once, like a type of blood? No, that isn't right, I think, but more as if I had already held them, looked into them. Dumbly, I am reminded of the women I've slept with, the women I've loved, rarely the same, as the train slows, pulling into another station along the way.

It must be a real small town, or at least a part of town that's well removed, because there is nothing but field out my window and, in the distance, some hills. Somewhere in the field, I believe I see the traces of a lake underneath the layer of snow that has accumulated. It has fallen quickly, I note, taking out some unfinished work and laying it across the dining car table. This should get me through the next forty-five minutes, just about enough to hold me over until

Binghamton. In another twenty minutes, though, we are still at the station and I'm pretty much done. I consider going over my work again or maybe asking someone what the holdup is, but instead I decide on trudging to the end of a book that I've been reading. After that, I'll make some inquiries. I glance quickly at the smoke that seems now to be marked by red streaks? I can't tell through the falling snow. The book ends badly and I put it back in my bag. Getting up from my seat, I feel achy all over. I stretch, lifting my arms into the air, and yawn. There are very few passengers in the dining car with me: a woman and her child a few booths ahead and an older man with a laptop closer to the back. Earlier, the child had stood up briefly and gawked out the window at the smoke. Minutes later, she was nibbling at her sleeve and playing some kind of game with her fingers.

I make my way toward the front of the train in search of an attendant or an operator or a conductor. Out the window, I try to get a glimpse of the station, but realize my car must be fairly far back because I don't see the station at all. Where had I gotten onto the train, which car? I can't remember. Here, passengers must have to get out from the first four or five cars, as is common at these smaller stops. I don't find any authorities, though, just people sitting around, half asleep or reading the paper. I head back to my car, and from there, I move toward the back of the train. As I do so, I come to accept the fact that we aren't at a station, really, but are in fact just sitting here, essentially in the middle of nowhere so far as I'm concerned. Now, I don't have any appointments, my sister probably doesn't even have a job, and—in general—time is not an issue for me, but I'm interested in getting some answers about what's stopping us, if only to pass the time now that my book is finished. And who knows, I think, perhaps I will catch a glimpse of that ghost woman from the platform again. Yet, the only person I can find is the man minding the other food car at the far end of the train. He doesn't have much to reveal. He says, "It all feels like a routine stop." Can he tell by the way the engine rumbles beneath us? Can he sense something in the way we pulled to a stop? Do stops that aren't routine bring a special feeling of unease, a tension in the air or thickness? I don't ask him any of these things, but instead buy a two-dollar water. He assures me that we'll probably be moving shortly.

He's right too. After I get to my seat, get through about half of that bottle of water and idly peruse the transit safety pamphlets for a bit, the train does get moving—backwards. We are headed back toward the smoke, I think, and I envision all the trains across the country suddenly moving toward this central point and then rising upward with the plume. In fact, however, we only go about thirty feet before we stop again. Outside, the snow is fairly heavy, and in here the air is beginning to feel a bit stale, stuffy. I loosen my tie, unbutton my shirt a bit. Over the intercom, a man reports, "Due to a combination of a minor mechanical failure and inclement weather, the train cannot progress on its own. We are waiting for another engine to bring us the rest of the way, which should be here shortly." The intercom clicks off. I think about the train being lugged along slowly through the woods and decide it best to call my sister, let her know that I'll be late—not that I actually expected her to be on time, though. Actually, I debate whether or not I should say anything; maybe we would even get to the station at the same time if she doesn't know I'll be pulling in late. I think better of it though, take out my cell phone, and see that there's no service. Of course not—we're in the middle of nowhere. You don't need a cell phone out here. There's no one to call. I think about making phone calls to trees, to hills and rocks, or them calling me—long distance in the middle of the night, in need of money, sex, or drugs. My sister never calls my mother, really, or only very rarely. It is her special talent to be busy on birthdays, working on Christmas, sick on anniversaries. Another of her talents is lying.

197

In the same way that I often feel unnecessarily close to my family, or at least uncommonly, my sister is unprecedentedly absent and apart. It occurs to me that I don't love her. Outside the window, I see a group of people walking into the field. One of them is the girl from the platform. I debate in my mind whether or not she is really someone I've ever met. I can only catch glimpses of her through the people mingling about—is she even my age? Or is she younger? As for that—how old is my ghost, my blueprint? Does she age? Or will she always stay the same, even as I grow older? Outside, the plume of smoke seems graceful almost to the point of motionlessness. It is hard to conceive of being farther from an imaginary woman who solely exists, or doesn't, only in pieces and parts. In a moment, a train operator comes breezing through the car and tells us to take a breather outside if we'd like. Feeling cramped and stifled, I take him up on the offer. Who knows how long we'll really be here, I think. Best to take the carrots as they're given. I toss on my coat and gloves and head toward the end of the car. The door is open and a set of metal stairs has been lowered to make it easier to get out. A woman and her child follow after me. Outside, people smoke cigarettes alone. It's apparent that no one on this train knows each other really, save for a few here and there. The snow is about six inches deep, and many of us have made our way underneath one of the few trees in the field, a large elm where some of the grass still shows.

198

In the distance the smoke still billows without any sign of stopping. I notice that, in fact, the black cloud is mingling with the grey ones above us. Somewhere nearby someone has a stove going, the familiar smell of burning wood wafting through the field. Through a train window, back in my car, I see the conductor talking with the older man who had been using the laptop. They seem to be arguing over something. The older man, shaking his head, gathers up his briefcase, puts on an old fedora and walks out into the snow with his jacket over his arm, annoyed or defeated. Despite the snow, it isn't very cold. The woman's child is running about without its jacket on. The kid is filthy, too, I notice. Had it been that filthy before? It must have been, I reason, because we've only been out here a few minutes and there's nothing but fresh, white snow. I remember, when I was younger, my sister wiping dirt from my face with a thumb wetted with her own saliva.

She does the same thing now for her own kids when the mood strikes her. Sometimes I see her wiping next to nothing away with her filthy thumbs as if out of nervous habit. It must be a type of new itch that parents get, just a feeling, something you have to respond to, rubbing your child's face. The only way to explain the careful attention of her thumbs—in light of so much neglect and anger—is to call it genetic. I imagine the volcanic wave freezing her like that, one thumb stretching her daughter's cheek into a pained grimace. Families would love that one, I think, would flock to it for the photo op.

A train attendant appears in the doorway of another car. He makes his way toward a larger group of passengers huddled under another tree. Whatever he is telling them gets a strong reaction. Someone actually stomps their foot. I feel for the attendant, who seems to be simply delivering a message, and think maybe these people, who are now looking almost threatening, should lay off him a bit. The attendant shakes his head, shrugs his shoulders, puts his hands up defensively, and then points in our direction. He reboards the train, leaving the people under the tree looking stunned. Will it be a longer wait perhaps? Probably very long by the looks of things. Great, I think. The train starts to move forward a bit, perhaps adjusting position for the new engine headed our way.

It seems to be picking up speed rather quickly, though, I think, and a few people are actually running after the train, trying to jump on while it gains speed. The conductors and attendants raise the stairs and close the doors quickly though,

199

and the passengers can only run alongside it waving their hands. The train keeps going, some crew members looking blankly out the windows at us, and then it pulls around the bend. I am surprisingly thankful that none of them wave.

It doesn't appear to be coming back. No one says anything. There's not much to say. Some people from the other tree make their way toward my group. Once they arrive, the talking bursts out suddenly from almost everyone, a chorus of "What's happening?" and "Where's the train going?" and "What about our luggage?" and "What did they say over there?" A man who had run alongside the train speaks up, tells us that the conductor claimed the train had become too dangerous for passengers. A leak of some sort, gas, and that we couldn't stay on the train any longer. The other engine would be here shortly, and our old train had to move in order to make room for it. There was only one set of tracks, I realize. We could pick up our luggage in Binghamton. The explanation makes just enough sense to keep us from acting out against the train company. Not that there is much we could do out here besides kick the railway ties a bit. Still, the conductor's explanation, although unnerving and unsettling and unsatisfying, is not totally ridiculous. If there really was a gas leak, maybe it was best that the train leave us here out of harm's way. What if it exploded? We were only feet from the tracks and would be blown to bits or torn apart by flying steel. Perhaps something similar had caused the smoke in the distance? Perhaps other people had been left in the snow as well. In any event, there isn't much else we could do but accept it.

Now, all told, there are about twenty of us here, and a pretty pitiful lot at that. Not a group you'd want to have your back in a pit fight. I spot a man pulling out a cigarette and sidle up to him for a light. I don't need one, really, but I feel like talking. He wears an old, tweed golfer's cap and a long beige overcoat. He's amiable enough, but not very talkative—and we stand about smoking for a bit before anyone says much of anything. Eventually though, he remarks, "I can just about see our luggage."

I try to imagine it myself—being carted off the train and ushered to a special area of the station. "Do you think they'll have a lot of paperwork to fill out when we go to get it back?" Puffing his cigarette, he grunts, "No, you're not listening." He points off toward some trees up the way. "I can just about see our luggage. My glasses are in my suitcase, though, so it's a little tough, but I believe those're our bags right over there." I strain my eyes against the glare of the snow, but it appears he might be right. At least, there is a pile of suitcases and bags stacked up pell-mell just over a little hill. Whether or not they are ours is yet to be seen though. "My name's Dan," he says to me, offering a hand. He's got a good shake, I think as I offer my name in exchange. Without discussion, we stomp out our cigarettes and start walking toward the baggage over the hill.

"You noticed that smoke?" I ask, our backs to the plume.

"What do you think?"

He's right—of course he noticed it. "Yeah, well, you never know."

"That's true," he says. "I guess you don't. Still, I've seen the thing. It's huge and reminds me of a wrestler." He sparks up another cigarette. "What of it?"

"That's it in a nutshell, really. What of it? I don't know."

"Well, I did a lot of wrestling in my high school days. College too, though I wasn't as serious. I always thought I'd get more disciplined in university, but I was totally wrong." He pats his belly, a paunch really. "I got this instead. Earned it just as much as someone might earn a medal." He laughs at the thought of flesh as a prize. "But in high school, I was a pro. Top form. And I had a rule: wait for them to make the first move. There's too many options otherwise. Worked every time."

Peering quickly over my shoulder at the black cloud, I notice it's gotten a bit bigger.

Dan seems to be finished talking. I mull over his anecdote a bit. "So...are you saying we wait till a tower of smoke 'makes a move?'" It's the best I can come up with.

"In so many words, sure."

"What kind of 'move' are you expecting smoke to make?"

"You never really know until it happens with these things." He puffs his cigarette resolutely. "Works every time, though." He tries to blow a smoke ring, but fails. I don't mention it—we're just coming up on the luggage. The pile actually stretches up around the bend, thinning as it gets farther away. Lightly dusted in snow, the bags look lonely but somehow not out of place, like a peculiar but natural bed of rock. Sure enough, there's my case and my bag underneath a large camping pack. Dan scoops one up as well, opens it and removes a set of glasses. Slipping them on, he says, "Much better," and rubs his nose, leaving a dark streak. How did our luggage get so dirty so quickly, I wonder. Heading back to the others, we don't say anything. Everyone goes into an uproar over the luggage, all sorts of shouts and worries and theories being tossed about, but no one mentions the smoke. A few men volunteer to go grab all the luggage and manage to do it in just two trips, remarkably. After a wave of frantic cell phone checking futilely rises and then breaks, we all wait patiently under the tree, getting colder. The woman rubs her child's face with her thumb. She examines her fingers and then stands up: "It's ash," she says to no one in particular. I put my palm out and catch a few flakes of snow in my hand. I rub my fingers together, leaving a dark powder on the tips.

203

Eventually, the snow slows, but the ashes don't, and soon it is only soot falling and blanketing the ground. It gets darker, colder. There is no sign of a train coming anytime soon, and at first, people talk to each other, but eventually we become quiet as if to save energy, and we just stand there silently next to our luggage. Occasionally, someone coughs. A younger man has the smart but depressing idea of making a fire. He gathers a crew of people to find dry kindling, wood. Soon there are a few fires going, everyone standing around one or the other to stay warm. Dan and I are at different fires. The woman from the platform is around the one closest to the tracks. At mine, the man next to me, an older guy, holds something out to everyone that he has caught in his hand. "Look," he says. It's a small piece of a document, burnt away down to the corner, but it is emblazoned with a corporate letterhead, a company's name. None of us have heard of it before, but we can all imagine the type of building it must have come from.

While we wait, we take to examining the larger pieces of material that float down from the sky. They come in groups of similar things, like flocks of birds or schools of fish. We catch pieces of newspapers, mail, high school essays, town hall records, family photographs. It's too dark to see the billowing smoke now, but we see a glow on the horizon, constant and red. I wonder if this is the first move—or if, when it does come, we will even recognize it. It's possible that a first move has actually been made long ago and that we have missed it entirely. I take a peek at Dan across the field and wonder what his countermoves looked like in his high school days. I never wrestled, but I think I'm not unlike him. I'm not an initiator. I avoid conflict. Meanwhile, my sister gravitates toward it as if by magic. She exposed her children to the worst people she could find. Something drew her to locking her kids in their room to "play" while she watched television, drank, had sex for money. A magic gravity. Dan's methods attract me, though, because they relieve responsibility. As together as I might seem—job, bills, education, all taken care of—I do avoid responsibility out of habit. I have only achieved it by trapping myself into it, by leaving myself no choice. I am reminded suddenly of a car accident I was in years ago. It was snowing then, too, like the ash falling here in the field. I remember realizing I had lost control of the car, and the serenity that followed. There was nothing to do but wait for the eighteen wheeler headed toward me to make the move. If I could, I'd live my whole life like that, I think.

"We're going to the next station," a young woman says, having approached us from another fire. "We're going to find out what the hell is going on." Through some of the smoke above, the moon glows, visible every now and then in the empty patches. I eye the girl from the platform, hoping she'll come over here to tell us something too. I've been waiting for the ghost to make the first move for a long time, and I'm not about to change it now. "If anyone wants to come, feel free. We don't know how far it is, but we'll probably run into something either way, even if it isn't a station." A few people join the effort. I debate in my mind whether or not to go. As those who are leaving gather by the tracks, I see the platform girl pick up her things. I decide to believe that it's no longer up to me. With no reason to walk in any other direction, we walk along the tracks. Most of us get tired. While we are setting up places to sleep, there is another explosion, to the north. It is louder and closer than the first, but still distant. Soon, smoke is rising there too. In the morning, our fires have dimmed, so we spend some time rekindling them. Before we get going, someone reads a book, another a magazine. One woman knits. Others check cell phones, but not frantically.

"There hasn't been a plane in hours, all morning really," someone remarks. There is an airport in a city not too far from here, I remember. We keep reading, knitting, sitting. I check my phone. Once everyone is ready, we get walking again. My sister is no doubt worried by now, my mother too. And of course, I am worried about them. Yet, I find myself unable to feel much tension at all. It's calm here walking by the tracks, very still. The trees are quiet, disturbed only by clumps of snow falling off the branches above. It is a beautiful November morning, almost cloudless. In fact, it appears as if the smoke in the south is starting to slow, to weaken, which somehow disappoints me, I note. I don't really want it to end, I think. The best part of my day is usually riding the train to work. I hate waking up and I don't like the job, but in between there? It's nice. It's all taken care of. It's comforting to be here on the edge of everything, really. There's nothing to worry about. We can keep going like this.

When we were younger, my sister and I used to sit by the window during hurricanes and watch, waiting for something to happen. It's one of my few fond memories of her because she left for New York at such a young age—sixteen. We were both fascinated by disaster, I guess. I remember it being almost erotic, the same sense of danger surrounding my feelings for the hurricane that would later be a part of crushes and secret looks at pornography. My sister's disasters were sexual, too: when she came back, she was pregnant. She didn't stay long. When she left again, she took a train—this train, the one I had taken. Our mother dropped her off at the station, let her go back to the man that had gotten her pregnant. From outside, while they waited for it to leave, she traced the words

I love you on the window. My sister followed my mother's finger on the other side of the glass. It is these things that remind me she is a person, I think, as our group comes up not on the next station, but a train. It is motionless, silent and leaning slightly into the curve it wraps around, tilted gently to the left. It is our train, of course—what else could it be? No others had gone by. The doors are wide open, the cars empty. They are cold, too, as if they had been like this for hours. We grab food from the bar car and keep moving. There are no footprints to follow, any and all long since covered by the snow and ash.

By noon, we arrive at the station. It is small, the parking lot made for no more than ten cars. We have to climb the maintenance access stairs to get up onto the platform that leads to the station doors because the way around to the front is blocked by fences. Inside the station, the ticket booth is empty. No one is waiting in the seats. The power is out, the televisions blank. I sit down and look out the window at the New York wilderness. I remember the last time I visited my sister, when I helped her move from one trailer to the next. The next day, I remember finding her in the morning, drinking coffee by herself, staring out the window, smoking a cigarette.

"This is my favorite," she said. "Just sitting here alone, looking." I looked out the window then, too. There was nothing out there, nothing particularly beautiful. Some dirty snow, a tractor, some sheet metal. Mud and half a bush. Maybe she saw something out there I couldn't. I wonder about all the

207

things she's never told anyone, and as I look out the window now, most everyone else bustling around in search of some kind of clue, I imagine my sister staring out her own window, alone in a train station parking lot or at home, waiting.

I think: Let the wave come now, 60 mph and silent. The platform girl walks by and I stop her. "Will you sit down here next to me?" I ask. She looks at me strangely, but does. I would too if someone asked. Up close, though, I see she can't be older than sixteen.

We don't say anything and I look out the window. No, now, I think. Do it now.

ACKNOWLEDGMENTS

Thanks so much to the following people for their support and expertise: Joe DeLuca, Natalie Eilbert, Tom Oristaglio, Mike Lala, Allyson Paty, Eric Nelson, Matthew Zingg, Will Aronson, Craig Savino, Brendan Rogak, Tara Lambeth, Kyle Hilbrand, Siena Oristaglio, Samantha Hinds, Carissa Halston, Randolph Pfaff, Evan Simko-Bednarski, John Cusick, Vicki Lame, Ronnie Scott, Lee Yew Leong, Molly Rose Quinn, Adam Scott Mazer, Roxanne Palmer, Jess Mack, Forsyth Harmon, Cetywa Powell, Gail Eichinger, Louise Eichinger, and Skipp Schwartz.

Endless thanks to the editors of the journals where these stories originally appeared: "Infestation" in *Armchair/Shotgun*; "How to Have Sex on Other Planets" in *Eclectica Magazine* and *SAND Journal*; "Kiss My Annulus" in *Contrary Magazine*; "Euclid's Postulates" in *[PANK]*; "There Are Places in New York City That Do Not Exist" in *Vol. 1 Brooklyn*; "Nuée Ardente" and "Anatomy of the Monster" in *The Lifted Brow*; "Plunge Headlong into the Abyss with Guns Blazing and Legs Tangled" in *Prick of the Spindle*; "Interior Design" in *A Thousand Words*; "Investment Banking in Reverse" in *apt*; "Cells" in *TRNSFR*; "Tuning Forks" in *The Litter Box*.

THE AUTHOR

Dolan Morgan lives and writes in Greenpoint, Brooklyn.

THE ILLUSTRATOR

Robin E. Mørk lives and works in Brooklyn, NY with her husband and their cat.

THE PUBLISHER

Aforementioned Productions is an award-winning small press and 501(c)(3) non-profit organization that publishes chapbooks, full-length collections of prose and poetry, and the weekly online/annual print literary journal, *apt*. Aforementioned is supported through book sales and reader contributions. Donations to Aforementioned are tax-deductible.

To make a donation to AP, visit aforementioned.org/donate.

THE TYPEFACE(S)

The font used for the body text in this book is Adobe Caslon Pro. The font used for most of the headings (except in two instances) is Verlag Compressed. The font used in those other instances is Univers LT ExtraBlack.